# Grid Search

AWARD WINNING AUTHOR
# E. M. SHUE

Grid Search

Cover Design and Formatting by Mountain Rose Press

Editing by Nadine Winningham of The Editing Maven

Cover and Interior Images from DepositPhotos

www.authoremshue.com

emshue.ak@gmail.com

*Grid Search*

Ryker Murphy has no interest in his family's vineyard. He has other aspirations in life—piloting helicopters, volunteering with the fire department, and working with search and rescue. However, his plans take an unexpected turn after a visit to the local elementary school for a fire safety presentation. There, he falls head over heels for the new first-grade teacher in town. Despite her carrying another man's child, he wants a life with the young widow and her baby.

Lynae Amberly didn't anticipate navigating motherhood alone in a new town would be this difficult, until she meets Ryker. The hot firefighter invades her dreams every night, igniting her pregnancy hormones. When he proposes a friends-with-benefits scenario, they're soon consumed by passion, blurring the lines between friendship and something more.

As their connection grows, shadows from Lynae's past emerge, threatening her newfound happiness.

Ryker is set to give her the world and her unborn child his name. But when Lynae goes into labor at the worst time and place, Ryker must use his extensive training to find and save them both. Meanwhile, Lynae is determined to protect her child from the looming danger, fiercely fighting against the forces seeking to rip her family apart.

To learn more about upcoming releases consider signing up for Consent for Suspense.

*For my bestie. My sister from another mister and my found family.*

*Trigger Warning*

Grid Search contains hot and steamy sex, profanity, some drinking, kidnapping, off page rape, off and on page physical abuse, graphic violence, murder and may contain other content that could be sensitive to some readers. Grid Search is meant for mature reading audiences, 18+.

When everything goes to hell, the people who stand by you without flinching — they are your family.

JIM BUTCHER

## Chapter One

### LYNAE

END OF APRIL

As I drive north out of Tucson, heading toward Prominence Point, I think back on everything that happened today. I'm excited by the results, but I still worry. Cherise Benedict doesn't make threats lightly. My lawyer says we've done everything we could, and that the divorce will be finalized in the next couple of weeks. The judge won't allow the Benedicts to file a motion to continue, but I still can't shake the feeling of unease.

I questioned whether the divorce was still necessary now that Sayler is presumed dead. My attorney thinks it's best to follow through, just in case he isn't, and it would keep his parents out of my life. His mom and dad are a bit on the crazy side. Not only did they force me at sixteen to marry their twenty-year-old son, but they had also coerced me and my father into signing an unreasonable and unethical agreement. They got away with it all because several judges on the bench are friends with Mr. Benedict. That's why my attorney had to fight so hard at the beginning of this process to get the judge we did. We needed one who would be fair.

Is it mean that I don't want Sayler to ever come back? He just wasn't right for me. I've tried to bury all the bad memories and remember the good times. He was once a friend. In the end, though, he hurt me and proved my point that love and marriage are just fairy tales that don't exist in the real world.

An hour into my drive, I pull my Jeep Rogue off the highway and stop for lunch at a nearby restaurant. Once I order, I lean back in my seat, letting my mind wander to the appointment I had earlier.

I sat on the examination table, trying not to fidget so the paper wouldn't make noise. Out of the corner of my eye, I watched as Cherise typed away on her phone. I hadn't wanted her to be there, but she insisted on being a part of every step of the process. It felt violating, and now I wish I'd fought harder against it.

Sayler's mother had never been kind to me. She would bully me into wearing clothes she deemed appropriate. She hated when I wore my cowboy boots or when I let my hair be wavy. She said it looked better straightened. The only compliment she'd ever given me was that it was a good thing I was pretty, claiming I was at least going to give her beautiful grandbabies to raise. That wasn't happening. Any child that came from this damn process would be mine alone, and she and her husband would only have visitation.

I hated that this is one of the concessions my attorney and I had to make. My body should have been off-limits. Yet, because Sayler was missing in action, and there was that ridiculous clause in our prenup, I had no choice. I had to produce an heir to carry on his family line, regardless of my own feelings. Thankfully, the judge had stipulated I only had to try once. If this attempt didn't work, as I suspected it wouldn't, I wouldn't be forced to keep trying. I was still in shock that clause was in the prenup. I had no memory of agreeing to it.

"Stop fidgeting." Cherise huffed as the door opened. "I don't see what my precious son ever saw in you." She grumbled as my doctor entered.

One thing I had control over was choosing my own doctor. Mrs. Benedict had hated that, but Dr. Kendall had treated me since I was a teenager and went on birth control to regulate my cycle. My doctor disagreed with this whole process, but I'd held off as long as I could. It had been almost a year since Sayler's unit was struck by enemy fire and he'd gone missing. A few weeks ago, we met with the judge. It had been decided that I had to give it one attempt.

I had very little choice over my body, while men and Sayler's insane mother told me what I had to do with it. I should have had a say, but because of a piece of paper, I had no choice. I was twenty-one now, and I still had no say.

My IUD had been removed the day after the judge reached a decision. I was immediately put on hormones to boost egg production. Four weeks later, I had been inseminated with Sayler's sperm. Through it all, Cherise had been there, not to hold my hand, but to ensure everything was done to her specifications. My doctor had voiced her concern, stating my body needed to adjust to being off birth control first. But Mrs. Benedict hadn't cared.

"Hey, Lyn." Dr. Kendall smiled at me before schooling her features and turning to my companion. "Mrs. Benedict." She flipped open the file, and I shifted again. Cherise's eyes flashed to me, and I shrugged slightly. "I'm sorry, but if you had listened to me, this wouldn't have happened."

I tuned in and shook my head.

"What did you say?" I asked, realizing I missed part of the conversation.

"That's impossible." Cherise stood up so fast, her chair hit the wall. "You did something wrong." She pointed at me. "I spoke with a fully educated doctor, and he said this was the process we had to follow."

"No, she didn't screw up anything," Dr. Kendall responded. "I told you her body wasn't ready. She'd been on the IUD for so long. It takes time because it had hormones too. As for my education, it's better than several doctors in the area."

I just sat there, processing everything.

I wasn't pregnant. I wasn't pregnant. The single thought repeated in my mind, over and over, as relief filled me. A smile formed on my lips. I was free. Grammy would have been happy. She would have said, "Dance a jig and move on, babycakes."

I jumped off the table, ready to dance that jig, when Cherise's next words stopped me.

"We'll be leaving and going to my doctor. She'll be going through another round. We have another vial of my son's sperm."

"No," I said, my voice soft, but Dr. Kendall heard me.

"What did you say?" Cherise turned sharply toward me.

I straightened my back, standing taller. Screw it! I moved to my cowboy boots and slipped them on. The heels gave my five-foot-three stature a little bit of height. I looked her directly in the eye and stared her down.

"I said no." The word came out firmly. "I only had to do one round, per the judge. I'm done." I took a step back and gave her a tight smile. I won.

For once, I won, and I kind of liked the feeling.

Cherise stood over me. "I'll turn you in. You'll lose everything." She'd used that threat before. She'd accused me of using Sayler's military GI bill to attend college, but I hadn't touched it. My grammy paid for my college education.

"Lose what?" I chuckled. "You threw me out of the condo. I'm done with school, and my grandmother paid for that. The military already told you they won't take away the other death benefits. You lose." She couldn't touch my inheritance from my grandma, which would be mine when I turned twenty-five. I currently received a monthly stipend.

My small victory was short-lived when she slapped me across the face, snapping my head to the side. Tears filled my eyes. I was not prepared for her attack.

"That's enough," Dr. Kendall yelled. She opened the door and shouted for someone to call security.

"I'll make you sorry, you little bitch." Cherise slammed her shoulder into Dr. Kendall's as she pushed past her.

My hand was on my cheek as I stood there with a smile back on my face. I couldn't believe I was finally free of her.

"Are you okay, Lyn?"

"I'm free." I nodded as I looked up at her. "I'm getting the hell out of this town and away from that crazy family."

"Good."

I walked out of the office. As I slid into the driver's seat of my car, I glanced over and found Cherise watching me. A shiver worked across my body, but I kept my head held high. The red mark from where she slapped me on display. Once I closed the door, I took a selfie and attached it to an email. I typed a brief statement, needing to document proof of everything, then sent it to my attorney. I also informed him I wasn't pregnant. He would add that information to the divorce proceedings.

"Here's your lunch, ma'am." I'm broken from my

dark thoughts and smile up at the waitress. "That looks like it hurts. Do you want a cool cloth for it?" She points at my cheek. My fair skin will show the mark for a while.

"No, it's okay. It's a badge of honor. I got out." I smile before taking a big bite of my grilled ham and cheese sandwich.

The waitress pats my back and walks off. I hear her say something about being proud someone got out.

---

Hours later, I'm looking in the motel room mirror. I reached Prominence Point a couple of hours ago and met with my new landlord. She's the sweetest lady. I'm renting a two-bedroom house on her vineyard. She even lined me up with a second job on the weekends. It's in her husband's fine dining restaurant, which is also on the vineyard.

Everything is finally starting to look up. This weekend was my graduation, but I chose not to walk. There was no one to be there for me, so what's the point. With my grammy gone, I have no one. When my parents were alive, they never came to school functions. To be honest, I stopped inviting them after they embarrassed me too many times. Sayler would come once I caught his eye, but it mostly bothered me. Now I'm okay with having no one. My parents taking me from my grandparents taught me to be on my own. I don't need anyone anymore.

Everyone other than Grammy just tried to use me. I no longer have to carry Sayler's baby, and I'm out from under his parents' control. All I have left to do is finish packing the few belongings in the apartment I used to share with Grammy. I also have to clear out the storage units I put my furniture and other things into while I waited to move after the Benedicts threw me out of the condo. I have six weeks left with my current employer, then I'll finally be free of Tucson for good. I work for a private school as a teacher's aide.

I need to let off some steam. When I checked in, I noticed the country bar across the street from my motel. Rosco's doesn't look the nicest or even the cleanest, but that's not going to stop me. I've never been in a bar before, unless I count the time I went to the country club with the Benedicts. We had to go into the bar to get Cherise. She was having drinks with her friends while they waited for us. Sayler wouldn't leave me in the lobby alone with his father.

Before Sayler deployed, he got us a condo near my college campus, moving me away from his creepy father. When we lived with his parents in their big house, his father would walk in on me numerous times. I was living in the condo when my grammy found me. When we learned Sayler was cheating on me, she started helping me get out of the marriage. That's when Cherise kicked me out of the condo. I moved what was mine into a storage unit, and then I received a letter from Sayler saying everything was mine and to take it all, so I did.

I look down at my outfit again, not sure if it's the most appropriate for this bar, but I don't care. It's not something Cherise would have told me to wear. Or that Sayler would have allowed me to wear, but I like it. The blue minidress is sexy and alluring, with its cinched waist and V-neck that shows the swells of my breasts. The country turquoise blue color is flattering against my pale skin. I bought it on a whim one day and was worried I'd never have the courage to wear it. I like prairie style dresses, and this is similar but shorter.

My butterfly necklace that my grammy got me after she found me is the only jewelry I'm wearing, other than my watch. I stopped wearing my wedding ring after I found out about Sayler's girlfriend. His mother demanded the engagement ring be returned to her as it was a family heirloom. I didn't care because I didn't need any more memories of that life. My long blond hair falls in loose waves down my back.

Tonight, I'm starting my new life on my own. Just the way I should have years ago. I'm ready for a life I choose. Maybe I'll date someone. Maybe I won't. Maybe I'll have a one-night stand.

I slip my room key inside my little crossbody purse and head out the door. I look across the parking lot and road to the bar, worried this isn't such a good idea when I hear the music and people yelling. But I won't let fear hold me back any longer. I push my shoulders back, hold my head high, and walk across the street.

The bouncer looks me up and down as I hold up my ID. I briefly wonder if I'm not dressed appropriately for this establishment. He steps aside, granting me access. I'm instantly bombarded by the smell of stale beer when I cross the threshold. This bar, like all in Arizona, doesn't allow smoking, but there is a haze in the air. I move to the bar, feeling eyes on me. The waitresses are dressed in tiny shorts and cut up half shirts. The patrons are in an array of different dress styles, most with a western theme.

"What can I get you, doll?" an older man at the bar asks me. His skin is weathered from the sun, and he has kind eyes but a lost soul.

"Beer," I say. I'm not a fan, but I know this isn't the kind of place to order a fancy wine like the ones Sayler's family used to order and have me sip.

"Bottle or glass?" he asks, and I remember some important safety tips that Sayler once told me.

"Bottle, no preference."

A bottle of beer is placed in front of me after he pops the top. I take a deep swallow and instantly don't like it. I try to cover my reaction, but the man notices.

"Sure you want a beer, doll? You look more like a martini kind of girl." He looks me up and down.

"I'm sure. Thank you." I smile at him, and he smiles back.

"Doll, you keep smiling at me like that, and I'm going to think you like me." He reaches across the bar. "I'm Gus. This is my bar."

I slide my hand into his and shake it. His hand is big and calloused.

"I'm Lyn." I can't stop the smile.

"You new around here?"

"Yep."

I turn to look around me at the dance floor. I practiced line dances with Grammy in our apartment. I so wanted to come to a bar and dance, but I never had the courage. Cherise always said only trashy people went to bars.

I sit there and nurse my beer, trying to get the courage to dance.

Men walk up to me and ask me to dance, but I decline. None of them attracting me. I don't know what I'm looking for, but I'll know it when I see it. I wanted to come in here and find out if everything I've heard about how sex should be is real. Sayler and I had sex only once, and it was awkward, painful, and traumatic. I tried to get him to stop. It's why I never slept with him again in all the years we were together. I came up with excuses and pushed him away. Grammy said it was rape, but he was my husband. You can't rape a spouse, right?

Part of me wants to have a one-night stand. I know I shouldn't, but I need to feel. I need to know there is more out there than what I've seen or learned from my past.

As I look around the room, a shiver races up my body. I can feel someone watching me. I don't know who, but I can feel it. My eyes finally settle on a man. His stare bores into me. I can't stop looking at him. He has dark hair that almost looks black in the dimness of the bar, but as the lights flash around, I can see it's a deep brown. We continue to stare each other down as the waitress moves toward him. She leans down, putting her breasts in his face. Jealousy hits me like a smack to the forehead. I've never felt like this before. I want to grab her by the hair and slam her face into the table. I want to tell her to leave him alone, he's mine. Not even when I found out Sayler was cheating did I feel jealous. This is a new feeling, and it makes me uncomfortable. My skin actually crawls.

I turn away as they talk, knowing she's more his type than me. She's beautiful and sexy, while I'm petite and just pretty. Sayler used to tell me I was like the girl next door. His mother always said I had good bone structure, but that was all. My father used to say I was beautiful, but he was supposed to say that. Wasn't he? My grammy said I was classically beautiful, with my cherub face and wide eyes. But again, she had to say that too. I don't see what they saw. My lips are too full for my face. They look like I use lip enhancers when it's all natural. My eyebrows are dark, making it look like I lighten my hair, which I don't. I'm a contradiction.

---

*Ryker*

As the waitress continues to push her fake breasts in my face, I lose eye contact with the sweet little morsel sitting at the bar. She's like a little lamb that's ventured into the wolf's den. I notice all the guys checking her out, but I'll be the one taking her home tonight. I know it down deep in my bones. The moment I saw her walk in, I knew. I'm the only wolf for this little lamb.

I watch as one of the wolves walks up to her. She denies him, and he walks away. Oh, yes, she already knows.

"Hey," I holler at the waitress as she starts to walk away. "Take a glass of the rosé to her." I point to the girl. By the cringe on her face every time she takes a sip, I can tell beer isn't what she likes. Plus, she's been nursing it for so long it's warm now.

The waitress walks off and puts in the order at the bar. Gus looks over at me and nods. I continue to watch as he walks to the back and returns with a bottle. All the bars and restaurants don't exclusively sell my family's wines, but they have them on stock. He pours her a glass and walks over to her. She refuses it at first, but then he points to me. She turns and follows his line of sight. Without missing a beat, the little vixen takes the glass and tentatively swallows while she watches me. My cock presses into my zipper, and I'm sold.

She pulls back from the glass in shock. She looks at it before taking another sip, then another. Smiling at me, she raises the empty glass in a silent toast before setting it down. For a brief second, I think she's heading toward me, but instead, she moves toward the dance floor.

All of the women file onto the dance floor for a line dance, even some of the waitresses. All of us guys hang back and watch as a Gretchen Wilson song plays, but I only have eyes for the beauty in the dress. Her hips swing, and that dress dances along her thighs, making me want to flip it up to see if she's wearing a thong or sexy panties.

Her cowboy boots match her dress, and I can't stop the chuckle because she reminds me of Rowdy's girl with her boots. Looks like I found myself a country girl too. She stomps her foot and bends, shaking her ass, and I'm out of my chair.

"Later, boys. I have a date with legs and sexy lips." I throw some bills on the table and make my way to the dance floor.

As the song ends, she looks over to where I was sitting. Her face falls with disappointment when she finds my seat empty. But then, her expression shifts to surprise when she turns and finds me waiting for her.

"Okay, vixen, let's go."

"Sorry, I don't just leave with strangers."

"I'm taking you to dinner so I can get to know you, and all of these other fuckers will stop imagining what's on under that dress." I reach for her hand and engulf it in mine, noticing how delicate it is against my calloused skin. She's a tiny thing, even with the heels on her boots. My six-foot-two frame dwarfs her small size. I wrap an arm around her and toss some bills on the bar to cover her drinks.

"Be good," Gus calls out as we continue past. "That little butterfly is sweet."

I look down and notice why he called her butterfly. Crawling up the back of her neck and below her ear are a couple of butterfly tattoos.

"She's safe with me." I look back at him.

"I don't know you," she says softly, and I stop and turn her to face me.

"I'm Ryker—"

She places her fingers against my lips, and I can't stop myself from puckering my mouth to kiss them. This little vixen is a sweet morsal I'm going to eat up.

"Can we just keep it at our first names, please? I'm Lyn." Her voice is soft and sweet, with a bit of a twang. I lean down to hear her, and her sexy, full lips are right there, so close. "I've never done this before."

"Only if I can have a kiss first." God, I need those lips against mine. I want her body under me, but I'll take whatever I can get right now.

"Okay," she says breathlessly.

I tilt my head and press my lips to hers. The warmth of her kiss hits me first, followed by the taste—a blend of the wine's sweetness and her lip gloss that I swear is something berry mixed with flowers. Fuck this, I need a deeper taste.

I growl as I pull her up my body and take her mouth deeper. She squeaks and opens her mouth. My tongue plunges in and takes over. Her tongue tentatively touches mine, and the action instantly makes my cock hard. I could drill her to the wall right here.

I deepen the kiss even further. When her fingers grip the hair at the back of head, pulling me closer, I'm sure I've got her now. I pull back and find her lips are plumper from the blood rushing to them, making them look pinker. For a moment, I wonder if her pussy fills with color like that too.

"Little vixen, if I don't get you out of here now, I'm going to embarrass us both, and I don't want anyone to see you that way."

"Please," she begs as she slowly opens her eyes.

I set her down and make sure she's secure on her feet before I lead her from the bar, which is cheering from our display. She's blushing and hiding her face. I walk out, and she points across the street to the motel.

"My car is over there," her sweet voice says.

I slide my tongue along my lips, getting another taste of her. I'm torn right now. I want her, but I don't want her to think it's just for a quick fuck. The more I taste of her, my body wants more than usual.

Yeah, I'm a bit of a man whore. I won't deny it. I pick up girls on a general basis. Unlike my brother, and now my cousin Rowdy, I don't have a woman or responsibilities. I just want to fuck the next willing pussy. But Lyn isn't that. She's something more, and I knew it when she walked in.

She rocked me to the core of my being. Now I'm floundering in doubt.

# Chapter Two

## LYNAE

**D**oubt crosses his face, and I wonder if I did something wrong. All of my insecurities rush forward, making me want to run and hide.

"If you don't want to do this anymore, I completely understand." I give him the out he needs.

He turns me to face him and wraps his large, muscular arms around me. My hands land on his flexed pecs. He's stacked with muscles, almost as sexy as the dark scruff on his face. His short, dark hair is trimmed close, along with his mustache. I've never kissed a man with facial hair before, and the tickle was almost more than I could stand. It turned me on, and I squirm again, imagining that beard sliding across my body in other areas.

Areas I've only read about in books. Not that Sayler had ever tried any of those things with me. He was what the books called a selfish lover. He'd wanted me to go down on him. The one time I tried, he forced it into my mouth until I choked and threw up. He got mad and yanked on my hair.

"Vixen, I'm trying to be a kind of gentleman here. I want to take you somewhere for dinner to get to know you. But I also want to see you writhing around with my cock deep inside your tight, little body." His dirty words do the trick.

"I know what I want." I drag him across the street to my room.

The door slams shut behind us, and he lifts me, twisting me around to press my back against it. I instinctively wrap around him, and he leans in close. I'm not scared of him. Something deep inside me trusts this man. I like him. His kind blue eyes make me feel at ease.

"Listen up, little vixen. I'll give you what you want right now, but this isn't just a one and done. I'm not doing that with you." His voice is serious, and I focus on his throat as I nod, making sure he doesn't see the lie in my eyes.

"Okay."

I'm glad I only have one bag, and that I didn't really unpack. I'll slip out and get away before he knows it. I want this. One and done is all I'm capable of right now.

He leans in and kisses me again, making my toes curl in a way I've never felt. Butterflies erupt in my belly, and I know if I were different—if things were different—I'd give him a chance.

He pulls back and slides his scruff down my neck as

he kisses and licks my skin. I feel a pull just below my ear and hope he's not marking me. When he reaches my cleavage, he sucks on the inside of my breast, really marking it. I thump my head against the door, loving the feel of his mouth against my skin. His hands are working their way up my legs wrapped around his hips. He pulls back and looks down when he reaches my panties.

"Fucking white virginal panties." He groans.

"I'm not a virgin," I clarify so he doesn't worry.

"Wouldn't have changed my mind, Lyn. I'm keeping you now. That little, wet spot and these panties sealed your fate."

I'm confused by his words, but I'm soon distracted when his long finger drags over the damp spot on my panties. I moan long and loud.

"That feels so good."

"It's going to feel so much better pretty soon. I'm getting my mouth on that soon."

He slides that finger along the side of my panties, under the edge, and pulls them to the side. I watch him as he looks down at my pussy. I'm fascinated by what he's seeing. His breathing increases, and I watch as the bulge behind his jeans becomes more and more pronounced. When that same finger glides from bottom to top, I start to thrash.

"Oh my God. Oh shit." Something stirs deep inside me, a feeling I've never experienced before.

I've never gotten myself off. I've never so much as touched myself. Sayler told me I couldn't, so I didn't.

I've read plenty of romance books. I know what's about to happen, but I thought it was all in the author's imagination.

Ryker's finger circles my clit a couple of times before gliding down to my entrance, where he slides it inside me. I slam my head against the door as I come for the first time ever.

"Fuck, little vixen, you're tight," he says, and then I feel us moving. He pulls my dress off and lays me down, leaving me in my panties and boots.

I'm lost to sensation as Ryker sucks my nipple deep into his mouth, his hand kneading my small B cup breast. I open my eyes to find that he's removed his shirt. I have to touch him. I slide my hands against his body, touching the muscles, feeling how they ripple as he moves around my body or moves me. I move my hands to his back and down into his jeans. There's a gap from him taking off his belt. His ass is hard slabs of muscle.

He kisses down my body, his beard tickling as he goes. I look down as he looks up at me, as if asking permission to proceed. I nod, and his mouth latches onto my pussy through my panties.

---

*Ryker*

Holy hell, this little vixen is going to undo me. I'm going to come in my jeans. She's so tight and responsive. Her amber eyes watch everything I do, and it makes everything I'm doing to her more intense. Makes it seem like we're making love instead of just fucking, and I like that.

Her essence bursts on my tongue, and it's a taste that is all her—flowers and berries. I rip her panties from her body and shove them into my pocket. The little virginal piece of fabric is mine now. She might not be a virgin, but her responses tell me she's not as experienced as she wants me to think.

I return to her sweet pussy, biting and sucking on her lips. She shoves her hands into my hair and holds me to her. I'm not leaving this heaven until she gives me a couple good orgasms. I saw another tattoo along her rib cage of butterflies and words, but I didn't take the time to read it. There is another butterfly tattoo on her thigh. Instant jealousy from another man being this close to her paradise almost consumes me.

I slide a finger inside her tightness. She cries out when I press on her G-spot as I suck on her clit. She moans and pulls my hair.

"Not leaving, Lyn," I growl against her clit, and she mewls as she moans my name. It's one of the sweetest sounds I've heard.

I slide another finger inside her, trying to prepare her for my cock. She moves her hands to her legs, holding them open for me. Her sexy little pink-tipped nails digging into her ivory thighs have me losing my shit. I suck harder as I push a third finger into her, and she cries out as she comes hard.

I'm up and over her, with my jeans at half-mast, sliding into the most intense heat I've ever felt when it hits me.

"Fuck. Fuck. Shit. Sorry." I start to pull out, but she locks her legs around me.

"Don't leave me. I've never felt this before. Please, Ryker, I need more. It's never been like this before."

"Lyn, I want to give you more, but I need a condom, baby," I tell her.

"Oh, I'm..." She pauses and then blinks several times, like she's trying to think of something. Please tell me she's on birth control. But then she shakes her head. "Wait. Shit." Her pussy ripples, and my eyes cross. My brain fries in that moment.

I pull out and slam back inside her. All I think about is giving her something that no one else has ever given her. Passion and orgasms. But she's already giving me more. Her eyes lock onto mine, taking in my soul, and I watch as she begins to fall over that cliff.

"Ryker, I'm scared." I notice the tears in her eyes as the passion builds up.

"Let it go, vixen. Take me deeper." I lift her leg over my arm, and she screams as she creams my cock with her cum. There is nothing in my head now except coming deep inside the hottest, wettest pussy I've ever felt.

I'm lost in the moment, and when I come a few

seconds later, she joins me, screaming my name again. I groan hers as reality comes back to me.

"I'm sorry, baby. I forgot to wrap it up." I regret it, but the bliss of where my cock is has me flexing my hips a couple of times, taking in more of this feeling.

She cuddles into my body, and I hear a soft snore. I close my eyes, taking a couple of minutes to relax before we do this again. We can talk about protection tomorrow when we are both awake. I like the feel of her body against mine. The after cuddle is one of the parts of relationships that I've always hated, but I kind of like it with her. The feel of my cock flaccid in her body as she's burrows deeper into my chest has me wrapping my arms tighter around her.

I wake a couple of hours later to a cold, quiet room.

"Lyn," I call her name, but there is no response.

I sit up and don't see her. The single bag that was on the table is gone. I double-check my wallet, just in case. It's exactly where I left it, with all the cash still inside. She didn't want my money. She just ran from me.

Well, fuck. I roll out of the bed and get dressed. I can't find my shirt, but that's minor compared to the fact that I feel like I'm missing something else. Something more important.

## Chapter Three

### LYNAE

**M**y body aches in places it's never before. I wish I could have woken up with him. My heart actually hurts the further I get away from him, and for lying to him about this being something more than sex.

It can only ever be sex between us.

I drive out of town and make it to Phoenix before the sandpaper dryness in my eyes forces me to pull over. I check into another motel and take a shower, washing Ryker from my body.

There's a hickey on my breast and a couple of love bites along my neck and stomach. There is also a huge hickey on my thigh near my tattoo. I wash my body, immediately missing his scent of leather, the outdoors, and musk. I step out of the shower and wrap a towel around myself. I walk to the bedroom, climb into bed, and fall asleep cuddled up to his shirt I stole. I didn't want to put on my dress, and since he kept my panties, it felt only fair.

A couple of hours later, I'm woken up to my phone ringing. I roll over and answer it.

"Hello."

"Lynae, it's Clive." Part of me wanted it to be Ryker, but I never gave him my number.

"Yes, Mr. Merchant ," I respond to my grammy's attorney. He flew in after she died and has been in Tucson since. I tried to talk him into returning home, but he told me my grammy would haunt him the rest of his days if he left me alone.

"I'm sorry to report your apartment and storage unit were vandalized."

"Dang it." I roll out of bed, and the towel drops from my body. I move around the room naked and stop when I catch my reflection in the mirror. Ryker's finger-prints and love bites are more prominent now that time has passed. He made sure to leave his mark. "I'm on my way."

I head out, returning to the hell of my life in Tucson.

W hen I pull up to the apartment my grammy rented for both of us, I find her attorney waiting for me. He walks over and wraps me in a hug.

"Most everything was destroyed. Furniture, clothes, and some recent pictures. It's a good thing we had most of your memories in the other storage unit under my name. Not only was the apartment hit, but so was the unit that had all of your furniture from Sayler."

His words stop me. Who would do this? Besides us and the Benedicts, no one knew about these places.

"Could it have—" I stop.

"I thought of that already," he says, knowing where my thoughts were leading. "We can ask, and I'll have the sheriff ask, but it's not going to look good."

"I know, but she threatened me after she assaulted me."

"I know." He wraps an arm around my shoulder, and we both wait until the sheriff's department tells us we can go check out the damage.

"How was your weekend?" he asks.

"It was good." That reminds me, I need to make a stop at the pharmacy.

When they finally let us into the apartment, I could cry. Everything is ruined. I'm going to have very little to move. It's a good thing the house in Prominence Point is furnished.

---

Two weeks later, we're all sitting in the courtroom. I'm tired of court motions. Attorneys. The Benedicts. All of it. I've had to move into the same hotel Clive is staying in after the apartment manager evicted me. He didn't want me staying there any longer after everything was settled.

Sayler's parents are practically trying to run me out of town. If it weren't for my job, I would leave now, but I made a promise, and I intend to keep it. So here I am, waiting for this to finally be over. For me to be free of the Benedicts.

I try not to squirm in my seat as Sayler's parents sit across the aisle from me. When the bailiff finally calls for all to rise, I stand up, and in walks the judge we've been working with for a year now.

The Benedicts have filed so many motions over the last two weeks, trying to drag out this marriage, but I'm not giving up. I'm no longer going to put up with being tied to that crazy train of a family.

Grammy and I worked too hard for my freedom to let them get me back now.

"I understand that no agreement has been reached," the judge says as he looks over the paperwork.

"No, sir," Clive and the Benedicts' attorney say in unison.

"I see that Ms. Amberley tried artificial insemination as part of the prenup, and you still won't allow for the divorce, Mr. Pikard?" The judge turns to the Benedicts' attorney.

"She purposely did something to prevent the pregnancy," Cherise interrupts.

"Mr. Pikard, please get control of your client."

"Yes, sir."

"Ms. Amberley, I see from your medical records that your physician made recommendations for treatment, but Mrs. Benedict insisted on doing it her way. Is that correct?"

"Yes, sir," I answer.

"Ms. Amberley, how old were you when the prenup was signed?"

"Objection," Mr. Pikard interrupts. "That has already been ruled on."

"Mr. Pikard, if you don't want to be held in contempt of court, you'll let me look over this situation again. I don't like that you used the motion that her father had the power of attorney due to her age and could sign off on it. She is an adult now and should have the right to decide whether or not she wants to get pregnant by a possibly dead man." The judge turns back to me. "Ms. Amberly, you are aware that by divorcing Sayler Benedict, you will no longer be eligible for any of his military benefits?"

"Sir, I don't use them. And to answer your previous question, I was sixteen."

"I find for the plaintiff. The marriage of Lynae Amberly and Sayler Benedict is hereby terminated. There will be no division of property, as each party will retain what they brought into the marriage. Ms. Amberly will keep her inheritance, and if Mr. Benedict is found safe, he will retain his, with neither party claiming a share of the other's. Mrs. Benedict, you will cease all motions and all contact with Ms. Amberly."

I sit here for a moment after the judge exits, taking it all in. Memories flood my mind. Being forced to marry a man four years older than me, someone I thought was my best friend. Sayler only married me because he had to join the Army to be eligible for his inheritance, a clause his grandfather put in place so he wouldn't "give money to a lazy man." I had to marry him because my father threatened to beat me if I screwed up his payday. The Benedicts had found out he owed serious money to a bookie for gambling on horses. He was the horse trainer on the Benedicts' horse farm at the time. My mother had already died. My father would have done anything to get rid of me because he couldn't use me against her any longer. He needed the money so he could go get drunk again.

Little did they all know that, four years later, Sayler and I would be getting a divorce. That he'd been sleeping with someone else. Or that, during our divorce proceedings, he would go missing in action and be presumed dead. I'm no longer the quiet, docile girl. I have money and position now. I have my degree, and up until a few months ago, I had family.

My grandmother swooped into Tucson a year and a half ago and took over my life, demanding to see the paperwork my father had signed. Now, I'm divorced and ready to start my life over in Prominence Point. I've been fighting for over a year to get out of the marriage. I need to get away from Sayler's family. His mother spent every day I was in their life breaking me down. I've tried to build myself up since my grammy came here, but it's hard when all you've ever heard is that your only value lies in your beauty and your ability to make babies. That I'm too stupid for anything else. The worst part is, I'm extremely smart, just not smart in the areas Cherise deems valuable, like fashion and design.

I graduated as valedictorian of my class in early childhood education. I've already landed a job as a first-grade teacher at Prominence Point Elementary. I'm excited to start this new chapter of my life. But I do worry a little about running into a tall, dark, and blue-eyed handsome man named Ryker. I dream of him almost every night and wake up panting for his body.

"I will make you miserable." I turn to see Cherise standing behind me.

"Don't worry, we already filed the protective order to keep you away from Lynae," Clive says, and smiles down at me.

"I should have had that baby. It would have been mine to raise."

I pause and look around the room, trying to figure out who she's acting for.

"Cherise, there was no baby, and if there had been one, it would have been mine. Not yours. Mine."

I turn my back on her, and Clive and I walk out another set of doors. I pray I never see her again.

## Chapter Four

### LYNAE

It's been four weeks since my divorce was finalized. In that time, I was notified that after more than a year of being missing and with new evidence surfacing, the Benedicts have determined that Sayler is dead. Funeral arrangements were made, but I didn't attend due to the protective orders. Plus, I never wanted to see them again. Instead, I took some time to mourn Sayler on my own.

I didn't expect to be sitting in my gynecologist's office so soon after my last visit. But after weeks of feeling sick and exhausted, I decided to come in when nothing else seemed to fit. I'm praying I'm wrong.

Dr. Kendall walks in with a smile that doesn't reach her eyes.

"Oh my God." My stomach lurches, and she hands me a bowl as I vomit. "I just got them out of my life. How did this happen? You said it didn't take," I say between bouts of retching. "You even did an ultrasound after Mrs. Benedict left, just in case, and there was nothing."

She nods and purses her lips. "I did, Lynae. Have you had sex recently?"

"Oh my God." I double over again as memories of Ryker flash through my mind. This time, my vision clouds over, and I feel faint. This cannot be happening. I was supposed to get the morning-after pill, but then life happened. What am I going to do?

"I'll take that as a yes."

"I did."

"Okay, let's do an ultrasound. Your body was still pumped up on hormones. Did you ever have a period?"

I pause for a moment and think. "A couple of weeks ago, I spotted, but never really bled. I figured it was just from all the stress I've been under."

"How long ago did you have sex?"

A blush crawls up my face, and she smiles. "The night I got the confirmation I wasn't pregnant with Sayler's baby."

"So about five weeks ago."

After a battery of tests, I walk out on wobbly legs, unsure of what I'm going to do next. Dr. Kendall gave me a referral for a doctor in Prominence Point, along with a prescription for prenatal vitamins and ultrasound pictures of my baby.

I need to find Ryker and tell him. I won't need him, but he should know. It's my fault this happened. I didn't have him put on a condom, and I forgot to get the morning-after pill.

When I return to my hotel room, I replay everything Dr. Kendall said and think about what I need to do. I have to watch my stress levels, and staying here isn't going to help with that. It's time to make some changes. I have the ability to do things differently than I would have before. Maybe I should take some time for myself and my child.

I call Clive and tell him he should head home, and that I'm leaving town tomorrow. My time with the private school is over. I had planned to stick around for a couple more days and then drive to Prominence Point to show up on move-in day, but now I'm taking some me time. I make reservations at a small but nice hotel in Phoenix to enjoy a little time in the big city.

---

My mini vacation was just what I needed, and now I'm settling into my new place. I was able to do some shopping while in Phoenix. I bought several dishes, pots, pans, glasses, and silverware from a discount store. Then I went to IKEA and ordered a few pieces, including a desk for my room, which will be shipped to me. I had planned to use the spare room as an office, but now I'll have to turn it into a nursery.

The doorbell rings, and I answer it to find a young woman standing there. She has long blond hair in soft waves over her shoulders. Her wide smile and kind eyes immediately make me smile back at her.

"Hello, I'm Isla. My mom, Charlene, wanted me to bring this down to you." She lifts up a basket with a couple of loaves of bread sticking out. "Dad and I just baked these." Her parents are my landlords and own the vineyard. She looks so much like her mother, I should have guessed it. Charlene had told me I'd see her around when she's not at school, and they have two boys as well. The vineyard is owned by the whole Murphy family, so there is even a nephew and his mom who live on a portion of the land. But it's so vast, Charlene said I wouldn't run into many of the others.

"Come in, I'm Lynae," I say, my stomach growling as the scent of garlic wafts from one of the fresh loaves. I step to the side to let her in, and she looks around the house before turning back to me. I close the door and start to walk past her.

"I hope you like the furnishings. I arranged them myself."

"Oh yes, I love it." I place the basket on the bar in the kitchen. My hand is drawn to the garlic bread.

"I can cut that for you. Just tell me where the knives are."

"Oh no, I can do it."

"Are you sure? Your hand is shaking."

I glance down and realize she's right. Shit, I haven't eaten much today.

"They are in that drawer." I point to where I unloaded the box of new knives I bought. Then I direct her to the cabinet with the cutting board. It still bothers me that I had to practically replace everything I owned.

The police in Tucson have no leads on who broke into my apartment and storage unit.

"These look new," Isla comments as she cuts a thick slice of the garlic loaf.

I accept the piece with a trembling hand, and my stomach growls. I need to take better care of myself.

She watches me as I take a big bite and laughs when I groan as the flavor hits my tongue.

"This is so good." I cover my mouth as I finish chewing, then take another bite.

"My father and I like to bake together. It's one of our things. He cooks all the time or manages the restaurant. But when I'm home from college, he makes time for just us. Same with my mom."

"Your parents seem really nice. I loved meeting your mom." Now that I've had a few bites of food, I can think more clearly. I open the fridge and pull out some cheese and meat. "Would you like a sandwich?"

"Sure. So, mom said you moved up from Tucson, but your accent doesn't sound like you're from there."

"No, I'm originally from North Carolina. I've lived in Arizona since I was ten."

"What do you think of Prominence Point so far?"

I look down at what I'm doing so she can't see my smile. I really like a guy here is what I want to say, but I don't. "I like it so far. I haven't had a chance to really explore."

"I can show you around tomorrow." She smacks her forehead. "Oops, I forgot I have to babysit my niece. I can show you around the vineyard if you'd like instead.

Reese is only five months old, but she loves walking around here."

"Sounds good. I have to drive into Flagstaff in the morning, but I'm free in the afternoon."

"Perfect."

We eat and get to know each other. She tells me she's in college for business management so she can help her parents with the vineyard. I don't open up much, but when she asks if I'm dating anyone, I tell her I just got divorced recently.

## Chapter Five

RYKER

## SEPTEMBER

I stare across the group of people and shake my head at my cousin Lance, who also happens to be my lieutenant. He's insisting I participate in the elementary school fire safety day.

"You'll be in full gear, with your mask on and air tank, so the kids can hear what you'd sound like in the event they had to be rescued. I'll be there too, but as you're the rookie this year, you're the star of the show. It's tradition." He chuckles, enjoying every bit of this.

"Yeah, whatever." I'm distracted when I spot Rowdy, my other cousin, walk out of the bay and approach his woman. I can't believe Rowdy finally settled down. His girl, Coral, is cute and reminds me of Lyn.

Ever since the morning I woke up alone, I've been looking for her. I go to the store and scan the aisles, hoping to spot her long blond hair. I can't stop wondering what happened to her. When I talked to Gus about her, he seemed protective and only said that if he were younger, he'd take a chance on her. I wanted to drag his old ass across the bar and deck him, but I didn't.

"Want to go to the bar tonight?" Flora asks me, and I shake my head.

That's something else that's changed. I haven't been to the bar much since the night with Lyn. I paid Gus and the bouncer to let me know if she returns, but I haven't gotten a call. Part of me wants to ask my brother, Logan, if he'd run a search for her, but without a last name—and the fact I want to keep our night to myself—I won't do that.

Besides, Logan's been helping Rowdy with issues Coral is having, and I don't want to distract either of them. Rowdy looks like he could be our brother instead of our cousin. It probably has to do with the fact that our fathers were identical twins.

A group of single girls who just showed up wave at me, and I turn my back on them.

"Nope, not interested." I walk into the station and check my schedule before making an exit. I'm not interested in any of the local girls anymore, and I don't want a one-night stand. I think that last one broke me.

When I pull up to my house, tucked away in one of the corners of the massive acreage that makes up our family's vineyard, I see my little sister's car in the driveway. It can mean one of two things: she's in trouble and doesn't want anyone else to know, or she's using my dock by the small pond out back. It's one of the few on the property, but mine is the best. I have it set up for water games and fun. I usually throw parties here all summer long, but this summer, I haven't felt like it.

It could be because I'm working two jobs now, but it could also be because I'm just not in the mood. As soon as my boots step onto the deck, I hear her.

"Down here," she calls, and I head to the lower level that opens up close to the water's edge and the dock. She's lounged back in one of the chairs with a glass of wine. Maybe I shouldn't have given her a key, but Isa and I have always been close. Our older brother's job was to keep the boys away by beating them up, while mine was to soothe Isa and reassure her everything was okay.

I can tell she hasn't been up to the parents' place yet by the tank top and shorts she's got on. Dad would freak out if he saw that much of her legs on display. Her shorts are tiny, and honestly, I'm not too happy about them either.

"What the fuck are you wearing, Isa?" I bark at her, and she rolls her eyes.

"When did you become the monk?"

She calls Logan a monk. Since his engagement failed and he ended up becoming a single dad, he hasn't slept with anyone.

"When you dress like that, I will be." I wave at her.

"Jeez, get over it." She sighs deeply, and I plop

down in the lounger next to hers, taking the wine glass from her.

"How much have you had already? You know you can't drink yet."

She huffs. "I'm less than two months from my birthday. Give it a break. Besides, it's too late." She reaches over the side of her lounger and pulls up the empty bottle of wine. "I've had plenty."

"What's going on, little sister?" I take a sip of the wine. As the sweetness of the grapes bursts on my tongue, an image of Lyn fills my mind.

"I think my friend Meadow is in trouble."

"This that girl you befriended at school?"

"Yeah. Her brother called her. He's gotten mixed up with a bad crowd, and now they're coming around our place and causing issues."

"I'll drive down to campus in a couple of days and help you out."

She reaches across the space and pats my arm. "You're the best big brother. Not a monk at all." Her speech is starting to slur.

"Yeah, yeah, whatever. Come on." I stand and reach down, lifting her into my arms to carry her to the spare bedroom.

"You're so sweet. You should meet my new friend, Lynae, except she has more secrets than the monk does. I know she's hiding things from me. She was married before and says she won't do that again. But I think if she met the right guy, she'd give it another chance." She giggles as she settles into bed and passes out. I set up

Tylenol and water for her on the nightstand before heading upstairs to the main floor.

I grab a bottle of water from the fridge and take a big gulp. As I look around my house, I realize how much it's set up as a home. It just needs a family. The thought bothers me because I never wanted a family until now. Until that night with Lyn.

———

Riding in the passenger seat of the firetruck on our way to the school, I look out over Prominence Point. The small town sits between Sedona and Flagstaff. As always, I think about all the times I've been offered positions in bigger towns, but I've always liked the small-town feel. I never had the desire to leave until recently. Now, I feel unsettled, and I don't know why.

We pull up to the school, and I jump out and finish suiting up. Lance heads inside to notify the principal that we have arrived. Once I have all my gear on, I make my way to the entrance, where Lance is waiting.

Today, we go from classroom to classroom, allowing the kids to check me out so they won't panic or run from a firefighter if there's ever a fire. The community council and school board believe that more kids are injured while trying to escape from firefighters in full gear, especially when there's smoke. So, we are working to desensitize the kids to our equipment. In some classrooms, the lights will be turned off or dimmed so the kids can see what a firefighter looks like in the dark with the reflectors on our gear glowing and lights blinking. They'll also hear the sound of my PASS alarm and learn more about the equipment we use.

We've gone through several of the older kids' classrooms and are now making our way to the younger ones. We start with the kindergartners, then move on to the first-grade class.

Lance opens the door, and I step into the room. The students are all waiting at their desks, arranged in groups around the bright classroom. I hear a click, and the lights go out. Some of the students scream, while others giggle.

"It's okay. Remember we talked about this," a soft Southern-accented voice says from behind me. It's muffled through all my gear, but something about it sounds familiar. I want to turn and look at her, but I have to stay focused on what Lance is saying.

When my lieutenant gives the signal, I get down on my knees and begin crawling across the floor, just like we do in heavy smoke areas. I push my Halligan bar ahead of me, and when I reach the first desk, I look up at the young girl seated there. She shies away, but then hesitantly reaches out to touch my mask.

"You're doing great, Ariel," the woman says.

Out of the corner of my eye, I catch a glimpse of black leggings encasing shapely legs and tiny, brightly colored Converse on small feet. Something makes me want to follow those legs up, but another kid touches my pack, and I get distracted.

I continue to make my way through the room. Sometimes crawling, sometimes walking. I keep my focus on the kids and not the teacher, but when another student gets upset and starts crying, that voice of hers is back.

"Oh, Gina, it's okay," she says from beside me, and I turn to see beautiful amber-colored eyes looking at me through the mask. Her full lips curl into a smile. "See, Gina," she says, reaching out to touch my mask. Long fingers on a delicate hand extend toward me, and the memory slams into my mind.

"Lyn," I say her name, and she rears back, almost falling over.

I quickly grab for her, steadying her as I stand. I shut off my air, remove my helmet, and set it on the child's desk before pulling off my mask and Nomex. She watches me, and when I finally see her face clearly without my mask between us, I want to yank her to me. Her mouth pops open in surprise. Her long blond hair is cut to her shoulders, falling in waves around her face.

I start to reach for her to sip from those beautiful, full lips again, but she steps back. That's when I take her completely in. The long sweater she's wearing fits tight to her body, showing a small swelling at her abdomen. I step back, my jaw tightening, as my eyes shoot sparks at her.

How could she keep this from me?

*Lynae*

I know the moment he sees my stomach. The doctor said because I'm so tiny, I'm showing earlier than some women do at nineteen weeks. Ryker is just staring at me, and I can feel the anger radiating off his body. His hair is sweaty and messy from being under all his gear. His blue eyes track every movement I make. I take another step back. When I hear the shuffling of my students, I'm snapped from the fog I was in. I have struggled with sexy dreams from our time together. I blame it on hormones, but when I'm this close to him, I wonder if I more than missed him.

"So, students, as you can see, he's just a man like your daddies under all that gear."

"Ms. Amberly, he knows your name." One of my students points out.

"He does. I know Ry—" I stop and look at the name on his gear. "Mr. Murphy."

Ryker steps close to me. "Mr. Murphy is my father. I'm Ryker to you," he growls low enough for no one else to hear.

Murphy. The name hits me.

My landlords are the Murphys. The girl who's becoming like a best friend to me is a Murphy too. She's talked about her two brothers. Oh shit. One of them, the firefighter, is named Ry.

A wave of nausea washes over me as my blood starts to race. I feel faint for a moment. When Ryker reaches out and grabs my forearm, electric sparks shoot across my skin, up my arm. I yank my arm away and unsteadily make my way to my desk. I stand there for a few moments, taking calming breaths, before I turn back to the classroom. The man who walked in with Ryker, Lieutenant Courtney, approaches me.

"Are you okay, ma'am?" he asks softly, and all I can manage is a nod.

I pick up the worksheets I printed earlier and pass them out, focusing on my duties. After a moment, Ryker walks back up to me.

"We need to talk."

"After school," I reply, silently praying I won't have to move again or lose the friends I've made over the last couple of months.

Ryker and his lieutenant leave, and I resume my class. When they head outside for their final recess, I sit at my desk and think over everything.

The past two months since I moved here have been amazing. I've settled into a routine. The principal wasn't happy when I told her I'd need to take maternity leave in February, but I reassured her I would be back. My second job found out I was pregnant last Friday when I got nauseous from the smell of meat they were cooking in the kitchen. I assured them I wouldn't be taking any time off.

I think about Ryker Murphy, and the worry creeps in that I might lose the new life I've started now that he sort of knows. He didn't ask if the baby was his. The look that crossed his face wasn't one of anger, but more of hurt.

———

I walk to the parking lot and spot Ryker leaning against my car, his long legs crossed at the ankles. Aviator sunglasses shield his eyes from the bright sunlight. As I get closer, he stands to his full height. He takes my large bag from my hand when I stop in front of him. I almost forgot how small and petite he makes me feel, but also safe. I never experienced that with Sayler. He had always made me feel unsettled and wary. It's why I left the bar that night with Ryker. I trusted him already.

"How did you know this was my car?" I glance around the lot at the other staff's vehicles.

"I have my ways." He waits until I unlock the door then places my bag in the back seat. "Plus, I asked the principal. I've known her for years."

"She shouldn't give out personal information like that."

"You're right. Like I said, I have my ways."

"Would those ways include your brother who works for the sheriff's department?" Isla told me all about her family. I don't have a family to talk about, but I did share a little about Sayler and his family, about my gram, and how I'd always felt like a pawn to my parents.

I watch as Ryker's shoulders tense, and his expression hardens. "You did your research on my family before you sought me out? What do you know about us? And if you think that by *accidentally* getting pregnant you'll get the vineyard, you're mistaken. There will be a DNA test to confirm I'm the father." His words are bitter and full of acid. I remember what Isla said, and I shake my head.

"I didn't know your family until I moved here permanently," I say, trying to keep my composure. "Your sister, Isla, is my friend. She told me about her two brothers—Ry, the firefighter, and Logan, the deputy sheriff. I'm not after the vineyard." I don't mention that I live on the vineyard. I don't want him to think even worse of me. "This was not planned. I know the baby is yours because I've only had sex twice. Once with you, and once with my ex-husband. It was all my fault I got pregnant, and if you weren't so upset, I'd explain everything. Obviously, this isn't the time. I don't need your money or anything else. I can take care of my baby on my own. I'll have my attorney draw up a release of your parental rights. You won't have to see us. I just want to continue living and working here, please. You won't have to acknowledge us. If you want me to stop associating with your family, I will. I was looking for you, but I wasn't sure where to start. Plus, I moved here and started working right away, so I've just been busy. I'm so, so sorry." I force the words out in a rush, hoping to say it all before my heart completely shatters and the tears start to fall.

I figured he'd be upset, but to accuse me of trying to

trick him so I can get the vineyard hurts. Tears clog my throat, and I push past Ryker, who just stands there, staring at me.

As I start my car, I look out the window at Ryker, still standing there, clearly processing everything I said. I barely make it out of the parking lot before the tears start to flow. By the time I reach my house, I'm sobbing uncontrollably. I'm thankful I made it home without causing an accident.

I turn off the car and press the button to close the garage door. All I want is to get inside and lie down. I'm exhausted from all the crying.

I stumble through the door into the mudroom off the garage and make my way to the second entrance of my bedroom. I fall onto the bed, curling into a fetal position. Wrapping my arms around my legs, I let the pain pour out through my tears and sobs.

I thought moving here would change everything. I thought I would have friends. I wanted to finally feel like I belonged somewhere in this world. I didn't expect to get pregnant. I didn't even plan it, but I wouldn't change that night with Ryker. He made me feel things I've never felt before. Desired. Cared for. Even loved, I think.

All of that exploded in my face when he accused me of getting pregnant on purpose to tie myself to this vineyard. I had no idea he was a Murphy and owned it. I don't need their money.

I don't know how long I've been lying here, crying, but my head is starting to hurt. My eyes burn, and my chest aches. A pounding starts from the living room, followed by the doorbell ringing repeatedly. The sound is making my head throb more. I roll to the edge of the bed, get up, and stomp into the living room, ready to tell the jerk at the door to go away.

Through the glass of the door, I see Ryker standing there, watching me. I stare at him for moment, wondering how he found me. What is he doing here? Just as that thought crosses my mind, my vision blurs and my head starts to spin. I reach for the doorknob, but my hand doesn't grip it. I feel myself starting to fall, my eyes fluttering closed.

# Chapter Six

## RYKER

I hate that I blamed Lyn for those things, but it's been my family's reality. Rowdy and Logan have both been targeted by women trying to get their claws on my family's money and land. Logan's ex even stooped so low as to get pregnant on purpose. All I could see in that moment was what he goes through every day as a single dad.

What makes me feel even worse are the things she begged me for. She doesn't want my money. She just wants to remain friends with my family. But when she said she'd have her attorney draw up the paperwork for me to sign off my rights, that's when my brain broke. I was completely shocked. I didn't even realize she had left until I saw the glow of her taillights as she fled.

I called Isla to find out where Lynae lived, and was even more shocked to learn she rented one of the cottages on the vineyard. I rushed over here, desperate to talk to her.

I pound on the door and ring the bell, fueled by the need to make things right. Lyn moves across the room, stopping at the door. She reaches for the handle, but then she collapses, crumpling to the floor. Shit! I can't open the door or break the glass without hurting her.

The side porch! It has French doors. I pull out my cell phone as I run toward the doors. They're locked, so I jump the railing and race to the back of the house. I can get in through the side entrance in the garage.

"Hi, Ryker, what's up?" my mother answers.

"Call an ambulance to the cottage Lyn is in. She collapsed." I hang up without saying more. I can call them myself, but I can't think straight right now. My only focus is getting to Lyn.

I kick in the door, and it bursts open. I rush inside, moving quickly to the mudroom. She must have been distraught when she got home because she left this door open.

I rush to the front of the house and drop to my knees when I reach her. Gently, I roll her over and check for a pulse and respiration. I catalog that she's still slight in my arms, but I can feel the subtle changes in her body. She's developing more curves, and I notice her breasts are bigger.

"Come on, little vixen, open your eyes and let me know you are both okay." I pull her onto my lap and hold her close.

She doesn't wake up, and I worry I've caused this stress. Her eyes are swollen, her cheeks splotching from crying. She's still in what she was wearing, even the little tennis shoes on her feet.

I gently rock her, monitoring her vitals for a few moments, until I hear a knock on the door. My mother is there, and I scoot back, allowing her to unlock the door and let the EMTs inside. I recognize them from the station, but there's no time for chitchat. I have only one thing I want them to do. Care for my family.

They are mine, and I promise myself I'm going to take care of her and the baby. Her words of only having had sex twice still ring in my ear. She was married, and they only had sex once. It shocked me too, but not as much as her saying she would keep my child from me.

"Ryker?"

My mother breaks me from my thoughts. I look up at her, taking in her mid-length light brown hair with streaks of blond. I remember my father saying that the moment he met her, he knew. She was his, and he would have walked away from everything for her. That's how I feel about Lynae.

"She's mine." I slide my hand to her gently rounded stomach. "They both are."

The ambulance crew takes over, but I don't let them take Lynae off my lap. I keep her close. When it's time to move her to the gurney, I lift her up and help them load her.

"Follow us, Mom." I toss her my truck keys. "Oh, and we need to repair the back door."

"Okay. I'll get your dad, and we'll take care of it." She doesn't question me. She knows how my father was with her. She's told us that she knew he was meant to be hers too.

---

Once we're finally settled into a hospital room, Lynae starts to stir.

"Wh-What happened?" she asks as she glances around.

"We don't know yet, but we are going to find out. You fainted."

"Ryker?"

I take her hand in mine as she looks between it and my face. "Yeah, baby. I'm here."

Her eyes flare wide as she looks up at me. Nurses move around us, getting her situated. One nurse starts an IV, while another attaches monitors to her abdomen.

"Ms. Amberly, do you have a doctor?" a third nurse asks, and Lyn turns from me to look at her.

"I do. In Flagstaff." She gives them the name, and I sit there, watching the monitors. The baby's heart rate is good, and Lyn's vitals are starting to normalize. But her blood pressure is fairly low.

"Ms. Amberly." A doctor walks in. "I understand you fainted today."

"Yes." She bites her lip as she looks from me to the doctor. "I might not have eaten as much as I should have."

"That could be one of the reasons, but I noticed that your blood pressure is pretty low too."

"I jumped up quickly after lying down," she explains.

"She was under a lot of stress, and I know she was crying," I add. "We had a disagreement." I hold up my hand to stop her when she starts to argue. "It was all my fault, a misunderstanding. We'll be fine from now on. I'm here to make sure that baby and Mama are taken care of."

"Mr. Murphy, what is your relationship to Ms. Amberly?"

Sometimes, I hate that everyone in this town knows me.

"He's the baby's father," Lyn answers for me.

The doctor nods his head and turns to walk out. My heart settles in my chest at her confession.

"I really did want to find you," she says softly, and I turn to look at her. "I was just nervous and scared. I didn't plan this." She looks down as she fidgets with the fingers of her hand I'm holding.

"Lyn, we can talk more after we got out of here. But you need to know, I didn't prevent this either. As the saying goes, it takes two to tango." I rub my hand across her stomach. I can't wait until I feel the baby moving.

"But it was my fault. I was on hormones before we got together. I had to try to have my ex's baby."

I rear my head back. "What do you mean?"

"His family had a clause in our prenup that stated I had to have his baby if he died or went missing while in the military, which he did. Before the divorce was granted, I had no choice but to fulfill the agreement. My attorney tried to fight it, but Sayler's parents had a better attorney. I had to do one round of hormones and IVF. It didn't take. Then I met you."

"Are you divorced now? Were you divorced when we were together?" My gut clenches at the thought of another man possessing her.

"I'm divorced now. Sayler was already missing in action, and I was only weeks away from the finalization when we met. But I was still legally married. The good thing is this pregnancy wasn't confirmed until after the divorce. My doctor in Tucson ran tests and did an ultrasound after the IVF, proving I wasn't pregnant then. They can't get their hands on my little bean." She rubs her hand lovely over her bump, and I see the softness in her caress and want that too. I interlock our fingers over her abdomen.

"We can do this together."

"Really?" She smiles, and tears rim her eyes again.

"Yes." I lean over and kiss her forehead.

*Lynae*

They keep me in the hospital for a couple of hours, monitoring both the baby and me. After a meal, a bag of fluids, and my blood pressure stabilizing, they discharge me with the recommendation I follow up with my doctor. We walk out into the lobby, and I stop dead in my tracks. Ryker pulls on my hand that he hasn't let go of.

Standing in the lobby are his parents and another woman.

"They're going to hate me," I whisper, and Ryker turns to me. "I didn't know you were their son. I didn't know Isla was your sister."

"They don't hate you, baby." He cups my cheek, and I slowly close my eyes. "It's all been a huge misunderstanding. But we will make it work. I promise you."

"You're sure?" I say as I open my eyes.

"Positive. They're worried about you." He turns and leads me to them.

His mom pulls me into her arms. "Oh, sweetheart, I'm so glad you and the baby are okay. We were so worried."

"I'm sorry." I can't help the apology falling from my lips. It's a habit I can't seem to overcome. I've always said it too much. I feel like things are always my fault.

Charlene leans back and smiles at me. "There is nothing to be sorry about. Isla said to tell you she's excited to be an auntie again and will see you in a couple of weeks. I'm just glad that Ry got to you so quickly"

"I am too." I can't say anything else.

Ryker introduces me to the other woman with his parents. She's his aunt JoAnna. She and his cousin Rowdy have houses on the property too. She explains that Rowdy, who is also a firefighter, is home with his girlfriend and baby. That Rowdy and Coral will come by to meet me soon.

I just nod and cling to Ryker. I'm overwhelmed by it all. I think he gets it because he stops everyone.

"I'm taking Lyn home. She needs rest. Did you get the door fixed, Dad?"

"It's a temporary fix, but it's better than nothing."

Ryker leads me out of the hospital to his truck, where he helps me up into it and buckles me in. He kisses my cheek before closing the door. I don't know what's going on, but I know we still have a lot to talk about.

When we pull up to my house, I notice the door is fine. "What door were you talking about?"

"The one into the garage. You were lying against the front door, and I didn't want to break the French doors. Wait for me." He gets out, and I watch him walk around the front of the truck.

In the couple of months since I last saw him, he's become more muscular, and his hair is a bit longer. I find myself squirming in my seat, thinking of his scruff against my thighs. I remember everything we did, and I want it again. My body is one bundle of hormones and need.

He reaches in to help me, and when our hands touch, there is that zing again. Every time he touches me, I feel cherished and cared for.

Ryker walks me into the house and sits me on the sofa. "My dad said he's going to have some food delivered. Do you want to get comfortable before it gets here?"

"Sure." I head for my bedroom, where I change into a pair of soft sweatpants and a hoodie. The air has cooled a bit as evening settles in. When I walk back out, I see Ryker closing the door behind him and a young woman from the restaurant walking down the porch. I know her. She's one of the hostesses. She and I haven't really gotten along. I wonder if she said something to Ryker because his jaw is set tight when he turns around.

"Is everything okay?" I ask as I pull plates from the cupboard.

"Nothing to worry about, sweetheart." He shrugs it off as he unloads the bag onto the breakfast bar.

I know there is more than what he's saying, but I don't argue. I don't want to stress myself out any more than I already am.

We eat and get to know each other. I feel like I already know him from everything Isla had shared, but now it's so much more. He tells me about how much he loves flying, being on search and rescue, and now with the fire department.

I need to share more about my past with him, and I try to think of something that's not going to make me sound pathetic.

"When my grammy found me, I finally felt like I belonged. My parents weren't like yours. My mother died from a drug overdose when I was fourteen. But even before that, she was only interested in spending time with me to make my father mad." I don't tell him that my parents kidnapped me. "My father died shortly after I was married to Sayler."

"Dang, babe, that sucks. Your grammy sounds awesome, though. Why did she have to find you?"

I look down at my plate and push the food around. "My parents never told her where we were. I didn't know how to contact her, plus I couldn't." I leave out the part about my father telling me she was dead. "When I saw her, I almost fainted. We were at the country club, and I didn't want to make a scene. Sayler didn't like her, neither did his parents. She helped me get the divorce from him. It tore me up when she died before the divorce was final."

"Why did you divorce? Not that I'm not happy you're no longer with him, just curious."

"I was forced to marry him. They paid my father for me."

"What?" His body vibrates with anger.

"It sounds worse than it is."

"No, it is worse. Explain."

I watch as he grits his teeth. It's in that moment I realize I don't fear him like I did Sayler. Whenever Sayler lost his temper, I was always the punching bag— verbally and physically. He'd apologize afterward, tell me how wrong it was, but he would still do it again later.

"Sayler said he was in love with me from the moment he saw me, but I think he just wanted to possess me. He was a spoiled child and got whatever he wanted. He had his parents pay off my dad's gambling debts in exchange for me."

"Babe, that isn't love or right. That's against the law. How old were you?"

"I was sixteen. Sayler was a friend at the time, or at least I thought he was. He had to join the military and left shortly after we were married. He was home on leave when Grammy found me. She tried to contest the marriage, but at that point, it was too late. So we got an attorney and filed for divorce. I discovered Sayler had been seeing someone else, so it wasn't that big of a deal. Until he went missing. Then Grammy died, and I was left alone with that clause in the prenup, stating I had to give Sayler's family a baby. The judge stipulated I had to give it one round. When it failed, I didn't think about the fact I was on all those hormones. That's when you entered. I'm truly sorry."

"Lyn, I'm not mad. Well, not anymore. It freaked me out at first, but now I'm okay with it." He takes my hand in his. I look down at it and then up at him.

Biting my lip, I try to find the words I want to say. "I'm glad it was you and not Sayler. I know that sounds bad, but I can't deny it."

"I'm ecstatic it was me too." He squeezes my hand.

I slip off the stool to take my plate to the sink.

"I got it. You go rest." Ryker takes my plate, and I glance at the sofa where my soft blanket is waiting.

I grab the blanket and move toward the French doors. I step outside onto the wraparound porch and settle into the oversized Adirondack chair. Wrapped up,

I gaze out at the mountains in the darkness. I love the quiet peace of this place.

"This right here is why I never left. I couldn't move away. I love how quiet it is and how peaceful I feel when I sit outside. My house is on the lake, and I sit out on the deck, looking across it at night. I'll take you there so you can see it soon."

I lean my head back and look up at him. He squats down next to me, and I look into his eyes. Something moves across them, and my heart clenches for a moment. I've never looked into anyone's eyes like this. I let him see all of me. The fear and the pain. He brushes his hand down my hair.

"I won't hurt you, Lynae. I promise."

Tears come to my eyes, and he brushes one away as it slides down my cheek.

"I'm scared."

"Let's just start out with being friends, then we can go from there."

"I like that." I nod and give him a soft smile.

He leans forward and kisses my forehead before moving to the second chair.

I feel my body being lifted, Ryker's scent close as he carries me. I snuggle into him. I must have fallen asleep on the porch. When I feel the bed beneath me, I stretch out and then roll over.

"Just lock up when you leave." I yawn and fall back to sleep.

## Chapter Seven

### LYNAE

Stretching, I feel warm and content. I slept so well. An arm slides across my body and pulls me into theirs, and I jolt upright. Turning, I see Ryker shirtless, lying on top of the covers on my bed. His hair is mussed up, and he chuckles as he tries to pull me back down to lie with him.

"Ryker, what are you doing here?" My curls are in disarray around my head. I reach up, trying to smooth them down. Since I cut my hair, they've come out more. The only way to control them is to spray them down and start over.

"I wasn't going to leave you." He slides off the bed, and his jeans settle low on his hips.

I lick my lips, lost in how sexy he looks. My body remembers everything he made me feel that night. I want it again. I pull my lip between my teeth and bite down a bit harder.

"Little vixen, you keep looking at me like that, and I'll stop being a gentleman and show you how to bite that lip." His voice has a husky tone to it, and my eyes drag down his body as I watch him adjust his cock.

"Holy hell." I gasp.

He leans over and pulls me to the edge of the bed. I rise up on my knees, succumbing to the moment. He takes my lips in a soft kiss, but then presses against them harder. I start to open for him when his teeth impale my lip, and I moan. My core softens, and my panties dampen.

"Fuck it." He pushes me back onto the bed, kissing me.

My hands are all over his body. Tracing his muscles, sliding over the dips and valleys. His hands are in my hair, holding my head, as he devours my moans and cries. I wrap my legs around his hips and start to move against his erection. I remember how it felt sliding between my folds, and I throw my head back as I moan long and loud.

"I'm going to fucking take you, Lyn." His voice is full of grit and desire.

He slides his hand under my hoodie and tweaks my nipple. He leans back and lifts my hoodie, taking it off in one motion, and then his hot mouth is on my nipple.

"Yes. Please, Ryker," I beg.

He moves to my next breast, and that's when my alarm starts blaring, reminding me I have work today. We both groan, and I roll to the other side of the bed.

"Shoot." I glance at him. He looks like he's about to grab me. His eyes are laser focused on me. I shake my head as rational thoughts return.

"We can't do this, Ry." My breathing is shallow.

He rises from the bed and walks around it toward me. "We can if you'd let it."

"Friends, remember?" I place my hand against his hot chest and push him away.

"Okay. Friends." He pauses. "For now." Then he turns and walks out of my bedroom.

I collapse on the bed with a huge sigh. That was so close. I almost lost it with him. I want to.

My alarm goes off again, and I shut it off as I head toward the bathroom, where I take a cold shower.

When I walk out, I expect to find him gone, but once again, he surprises me. He's standing in the kitchen with a mug of coffee in hand, leaning casually against the counter, his long legs crossed at the ankles. I can't help but take him all in. Every long, lean muscle of him. I'm in hell. I watch as he stands to his full height and sets the mug down on the counter. My breath hitches as he moves across the room toward me. My hands suddenly feel clammy. My core is throbbing, and I can feel my clean panties dampen.

"Little vixen, I'm going to get into that tight pussy again. Even if it's only as friends with benefits." He leans down and kisses my forehead, and I'm disappointed it wasn't my lips. He turns away from me and heads for the sofa, where he grabs his shirt and pulls it over his head. "I'm on shift at the fire station tonight, so I won't be able to come over later. But I'll make sure that food gets delivered."

I shake the sexy thoughts from my head. "I have to work at my second job tonight."

"You don't need a second job. I'll see you tomorrow."

He turns and walks out the door, and I'm left bereft and wanting. I wonder if he left me like this on purpose, because I'm not going to last much longer if he keeps this up.

---

*Ryker*

It's been a couple of days since I last saw Lynae. After my shift, she came up with excuses as to why I couldn't come over. I know she's trying to keep her distance from me, but I'm not going to let that happen.

I'm off this weekend, which makes it the perfect time to take her to my house. I also want to take Lyn shopping for baby things. She told me she hasn't found out the baby's gender yet, but we can find out together at her appointment next week.

I head through the back door of the restaurant that leads into the kitchen.

"Hey, Dad," I greet him, and he fist-bumps me as he works on something at the large stove. "Thought you had a head chef for this instead of you doing it?"

"I do, but sometimes I like to get in here and test out new dishes."

I lean back against the counter and watch him. He's just as tall as my brother and me. We get our dark hair from him, but he's got gray in his beard. I used to love watching him cook. He leads a kitchen like Logan and I lead on our jobs, completely in control. Nothing ever fazes him. He taught us patience when working with other people.

"Dad, did you have a hard time getting Mom to agree to be yours when you first met?"

He chuckles and looks over his shoulder at me. "Lyn giving you issues?"

"Only I call her Lyn," I growl.

"Too late, son. Everyone calls her that. You come up with your own nickname for her. And to answer your question, yes. Your mother gave me a hell of a run. In the beginning, she was so focused on school and getting a job that she didn't care about me. I had to prove to her I was hers too. Lyn has been hurt."

"How do you know?" I know because she told me, but it was like pulling teeth to get that much out of her.

"You can see it. She's alone in this world. Show her that she's a part of a family now. How about we hold a family barbecue this weekend?"

"Sounds good."

"Order up," he calls out.

"Thanks, Jaden." Lyn's voice breaks through my thoughts, and I whip my head up.

She's standing there in skintight black pants and a black shirt that doesn't hide her baby bump or her full breasts. Her black apron is tied over the swell of our child.

"Ly, what are you doing here?" I bark at her, and she turns around to see me.

"Oh shoot." She bites that lip, and I can't stop my legs from moving.

Ever since I had her under me on Wednesday, I can't stop thinking about getting her there again.

"Stop." She holds up a hand, and I walk until it's pressed into my chest. "Let me take this out, and I'll be right back in. I can't believe you came here to stop me from working." She shakes her head, and I turn to look at my dad as he chuckles.

"I didn't know she worked here." I defend myself. "I told her to quit her second job."

"Don't make her quit," my dad begs. He struggles to find good workers.

"I'll see. She shouldn't be on her feet that much, between school and here."

"She only works every Friday and every other Saturday."

"I'll talk to her."

She returns a moment later and drags me to the side, away from everyone.

"I know you want me to quit, but I like working

here. However, now that I know your girlfriend works here too, I'll quit if you want me to."

I shake my head, unsure I heard her correctly. "Girlfriend? Yeah, my girlfriend works here. I told her to quit because she shouldn't be on her feet that much."

"What? Your girlfriend is pregnant too. Don't you wrap that shit up?" Fire bursts in her eyes, and I'm turned on until I register what she said.

"I'm talking about you. You're the only woman I've taken bare. You're my girlfriend."

"I'm your friend." Her hands land on her hips, and I push her against the wall behind us and press my body into hers.

"You are my friend and a girl. My girlfriend. Feel that," I growl into her ear. "Only you get me that fucking hard. Only you make me feel out of control." I nip her earlobe. "You are my girlfriend."

"No, I'm not. Tonya told me she was your girlfriend. When I came to work yesterday to cover for another server, she cornered me and told me she was your girlfriend, and that it didn't matter if I had your baby."

I rear back. "That fucking bitch." I walk out of the kitchen with Lynae chasing after me.

"Not in the main room, Ry. Don't scare away my guests." My father barks from behind me. He overheard part of our conversation and knows what's going to happen.

I stomp to the hostess station. I turn to see my dad still behind us. "You got her, please?" I nod to Lyn, and he nods his head. I watch as he pulls Lyn back. When she starts to struggle, I soften my brow, knowing I'm upset. "Babe, stay with my dad. I'm just going to clarify something."

"No, Ry, I don't want to interfere in your relationship."

I look over her head, knowing I can't keep my promise not to hurt her if I keep this from her. "Dad, can you follow us out?"

When I turn back, I find Tonya watching me. A look of hatred passes over her face when she looks at Lynae and then to her stomach.

"Outside. Let's go." I direct her out of the restaurant so we won't be airing this in front of the customers.

"Honey, we can talk after work. You didn't have to come by and see me, but it's sweet." Tonya's voice is full of sugary sweetness and seduction, but it does nothing for me.

"Out." I point to the door. She walks out the front door, and my father follows with Lyn at his side.

As soon as the door is closed behind us, I look at Tonya and then back to my woman. There are tears in Lyn's eyes and it guts me. "Lyn, I've never dated this woman. She's asked me out several times, but I've never dated her, not once. I swear. Remember what I promised," I tell her and then turn to Tonya.

"You're fired. You lied to the mother of my child." Tonya's eyes flare wide as she looks at Lynae's stomach and then back to me.

"Wait, that's really your baby?" Tonya sputters.

"It is. Now, get off our property."

She pulls her shoulders back. "You can't fire me, only Jaden can."

I watch as my dad bristles from her calling him by his first name. Only a few people call him Jaden, most here call him Mr. Murphy or Chef Murphy. Lyn, I noticed, is among the few.

"My son told you you're fired. Don't make me have you removed from the property. I don't employ liars."

"But, sir."

"No."

"You bitch." She rounds on Lynae, and I've had enough.

"Get in your car and get off this property now, or I'll tell every business in this town that you're unemployable. This is on you. Lynae had nothing to do with this. You did it."

"But, Ryker, we could be so good together." She turns the sugar back on, and this time she tries to add tears, but they don't faze me like Lyn's do.

"I'm only good with one person, and that's Lynae. Now, leave."

I watch Tonya storm to her car before I turn back to face Lynae. "I swear I never had relations with her at all. Not even a shake of the hand."

"Really?" I watch as the tension leaves her body.

I move toward her, and my father turns and heads back into the restaurant.

"Really, baby." I take her into my arms and tip her head back so I can place a soft kiss on her lips. "I think that's enough stress for the day. Tell my dad you're leaving so we can get out of here."

She shakes her head. "No, I have a shift to fulfill. I'll see you at my house after work."

"Not happening." I follow her back inside and sit in the kitchen, helping my dad when he needs it. After she finishes her shift, I follow her home.

## Chapter Eight

### LYNAE

**S**itting in Ryker's truck, I'm still shocked by what happened tonight. I can't believe he fired Tonya. I'm glad I don't have to worry about him cheating on me like Sayler did. Not that I wasn't glad Sayler was finding sex somewhere else, but I don't want that with Ryker.

I've struggled with my emotions since last night when Tonya told me she was dating Ryker. My heart hurt, and I was pissed, but now I'm relieved and upset with myself for believing it. He watched me all night tonight and hasn't left my side.

He followed me back to my house, where we left my car. Now, we are crossing the vineyard to where his house is located. When he pulls up, I remember seeing this house from across the lake during one of my walks with Isla. He parks, and I glance around, noticing how the stars reflect off the calm lake. He walks around the truck and opens my door. I reach out my hand for him to help me out, but he bypasses it and grabs me around my waist. He lifts me out and sets me on the ground next to him. I love how small and petite I feel beside him. He takes my hand and leads me up a set of stairs to the front door. It opens into a large room, beautifully decorated in soft grays and creams. The walls are a slightly bluer shade of gray, and I'm shocked by how homey and comfortable it all feels.

"Wow."

"Yeah, my mom and Isla decorated it after it was built. Are you hungry?" He walks to the large kitchen in the open concept area, and I shake my head.

"Your dad fed me well. I'm fine."

"Come on, I'll show you around."

He takes my hand and leads me upstairs. There are two bedrooms up here, one bathroom, and a loft that overlooks the living room below us. He then shows me the downstairs. There's a room decorated in a soft blue, with floral accents.

"This is Isla's spare room. She stays here a lot."

"Oh, okay." I smile as we move on.

I glance around the large game room. It has a huge television, a sectional sofa, and a pool table. He guides me outside next, and the lake is right there, with a boat tied to a dock.

"This place is amazing."

"Come on. I have one more room to show you." He tugs on my hand, and we head back inside. As we turn down the hall, he points out a small bathroom and the laundry room. Ryker stops at a door, then turns to face me. "This is our room."

"Ours?" I look at him.

"When you realize I'm not going away—and that we are meant to be together forever—you'll move in."

He opens the door, and I'm overwhelmed with emotion. "Ryker, we can't do this just because we are having a baby together." The room is dominated by a large bed and done up in soft gray colors.

Ryker turns me to face him before dropping to his knees in front of me. My breath catches.

"Ly, I know you just got out of an awful marriage, so I'm not going to push. But expect me to ask you several times, because I want our child to be born into our family." He takes my hands in his and kisses the backs of them. "I care about you a lot. I knew the moment I saw you across that bar, you were mine. I tried to find you, so the baby has nothing to do with how I feel." He kisses my bump, then rises. "I don't expect a yes yet." He kisses my forehead before turning to walk out the door, leaving me alone in the room.

I walk to the bed, barely able to step up to sit on it. I look around the room, replaying his words in my head. I want a family. That's all I've ever wanted. But he didn't say he loves me, and I'm scared to trust my feelings yet.

When Ryker takes me home, he walks me to the door and kisses me softly on the lips.

"I'll see you tomorrow. We're shopping in Flagstaff

for baby stuff, and then Sunday is dinner at my parents'."

"Um." I want to tell him no, but I can't. "Okay."

"Lock up, little vixen." He watches me from beside his truck.

I step inside my house, feeling so lonely, and lock the door behind me before heading to my room for the night.

---

*Ryker*

We pull up to my parents' house, where I grew up, and I see everyone is already here. Lynae tried to talk me out of bringing her, but I wouldn't hear it. She's trying to put up those walls again, but I won't let her. She's wearing a heather gray dress with a denim shirt tied over her baby bump.

I walk around the truck and help her down. Every day, I check on her. We went shopping yesterday and got baby furniture for my house. She keeps saying she needs some for her house, but I ignore it every time. She'll be living with me and married to me before this baby comes. I have at least twenty more weeks to convince her to marry me. I'm taking my dad's advice and giving her a family. I'm also not pushing her for sex, but I can't wait to get back inside her.

Her hand in mine feels perfect as I lead her inside.

"Mom, we're here," I holler, and she comes around the corner from the kitchen. It's been a habit since I moved out to announce when I'm home. Even though I don't live far from them, it still feels like coming home when I step through these doors.

"Hey, kiddo." She walks over and takes me in her arms. "Hello, Lyn." She smiles softly at her and pulls her in for a hug. My mom is a couple of inches taller than my woman. I love how my family is with her. Isla comes around the corner, and she pulls her in for a hug too.

"Hey, girl." She looks at Lyn. "Can I?" She points at her stomach, and Lynae laughs as she nods. My sister rubs her stomach and leans down to it. "I'm your auntie."

I turn Lyn to face my brother when he steps inside from the back deck, followed by Lance. I see Dad working at the smoker and grill.

"Lynae, this is my brother, Logan, and his daughter, Reese." Reese reaches for me, and I take her. "And you remember Lance from fire safety day."

"Nice to meet you," Lyn says as she shakes my brother's hand. "She's beautiful." She turns to Lance. "Nice to see you again, Lieutenant Courtney."

"Call me Lance." He laughs.

"He's both my boss and my cousin on my mom's side," I clarify, noticing the question in her eyes.

"Do you know what you're having yet?" Isla asks, and we both turn to her.

"We'll find out tomorrow," Lyn says softly.

"So it's true?" Rowdy laughs as he steps into the room, leading his girl and her son.

"Yes, I told you." His mom Gibbs smacks him. She's notorious for doing that to us boys.

"Yeah, but I thought you meant he was going to adopt him, like I am Archer."

"No, it's my kid in her belly, asshole," I argue with him.

"Ryker, mouth." My mom raises her voice.

"Yes, ma'am." I turn back to Rowdy. "Lynae, this is my cousin Rowdy, his girl, Coral, and their son, Archer."

"Wow, there are a lot of babies here."

"Yep, I can't wait until I have one," Isla says, and four pairs of eyes focus on her.

"Over our dead bodies," I proclaim, with Rowdy, Logan, and Lance agreeing.

"Now, boys, you know she's an adult now. I mean, she's the same age as Lynae and Coral," JoAnna adds.

"No, she isn't. Lyn is twenty-two. Isla is only twenty."

"I was twenty-one when we got pregnant." Lyn chuckles as she rubs her stomach.

"Don't make me take you home and spank you, vixen," I growl into her ear, making her tremble. Her body wants me, but her mind keeps stopping her.

We follow everyone out to the patio, where Dad is putting food on the table.

We sit down and enjoy a meal together. We haven't

done this in months. I hope we can continue so Lyn can see the big family she will be getting.

"Next weekend, don't you guys have tower training?" Logan asks as he returns from laying Reese down. He and Reese live here with our parents while his house is being finished. He'll have a place across the lake from mine. Eventually, Isla will build there too.

Rowdy's place is up above all ours and looks down at the vineyard. It's the property he and his mother chose. Because his father died when Rowdy was a baby, they moved home, and Aunt JoAnna built her house up there. She was still dealing with the loss of her husband at the time, and because my dad and he were twins, she didn't want to see my dad as much. I understand. If I lost Lyn, I'd want to be away from everyone too, especially if she had an identical twin. I never got to meet Uncle Jared. My brother did, but he only has a few memories because he was so young.

"Yeah, we do," I answer. "Why?"

"Just wondering when you all will be able to help me move. The house should be done this next week."

"Your house is the one across the lake from Ryker's, right?" Lynae asks, and I can't wait until she says, "ours."

"Yep."

"Oh, Logan, when will you be able to start interviewing those nannies?" My mother interrupts our conversation.

"Let me get moved in first."

"Okay."

"Speaking of which," I say, "how about Sunday?"

"Sounds good."

---

A couple of hours later, we pull into Lynae's driveway. I hate dropping her off and wish she were coming home with me instead. She smiles at me as I reach in to help her out.

"I loved spending time with your family. Thank you for inviting me."

"Of course. You'll go with me next month when we do it again."

"Oh, I don't want to overstay my welcome. Plus, that's so far off."

"Come on, baby." I walk her into the house and wait for her as she changes into something more comfortable.

I have the movie queued up that we are going to watch to relax. I talked her into letting me stay for a movie, seeing as she doesn't have to work tomorrow. It's a teacher in-service day, and she has her appointment.

"What time will you be here tomorrow?" she asks, and I almost swallow my tongue when I turn to face her.

She's wearing loose-fitting pink pajama pants and a sleeveless top that crosses over itself, opening to allow her to nurse after the baby is born. All I can think about is getting my mouth around those rosy nipples again.

She settles on the sofa, leaving space between us, but I'm not having that. I pull her into my body, and she snuggles in as we start the movie.

After a few moments, I notice she's squirming. As for me, I'm having a hard time just sitting here with her fresh, floral scent washing over me. My mouth waters, wanting to get between her legs again. It's been so long since I've had her essence on my tongue, and my body is primed for her right now. She squirms again, shifting her legs, and I look down at her. Her nipples are pebbled behind her shirt, and I know what her problem is.

"Baby, you okay?" I ask, hearing the gruffness in my voice.

Her head lolls back on my arm, and she looks up at me. I can see the need in her eyes. I lean down and take her lips in a thorough kiss. Before I know it, I have her on her back, and I'm over her body. Her legs open, and I nestle into her core. I can feel the heat radiating from her sweet pussy through our clothes. I pull away from her lips, and they are nice and swollen. I slide open her shirt and see her breasts behind the soft sleep bra she's in. I pull it up to expose her rosy nipples. The small buds harden from the cool air in the room. I lean down and take one in my mouth. I move to her other and lave it, sucking it deep, until she's moving under me.

My hand slides down her belly and into her sleep pants. She arches, urging me to move my hand to her core faster.

"Relax, sweetheart, I've got you."

My fingers slide into her panties, and she's soaked. I almost bust a nut in my jeans, she's so hot and wet. Slipping a finger between her folds, I bypass her clit and go for her core, where I bury my finger in her tight heat.

"Yes, please, Ryker."

I lean back down and suck her nipple into my mouth again as I fuck her with my finger. I add a second, and when she starts to tighten around them, I use my thumb to rub her clit. She rips her mouth from mine and moans long as she comes.

"Fuck, baby, I need inside you."

"I—" She pauses, and I know I'm going home to take a cold shower.

"It's too soon. I know." I pull my fingers from her core and lick them clean, watching as her eyes dilate.

I stand up and adjust myself as I look down at her. I left a small hickey on her breast, and they are still shiny from my mouth. Her pants are partially down, but she's still covered.

"I better go, or I'm going to talk you into letting me fuck you."

She bites her lip and nods as she fixes her clothes.

After I watch her lock herself in, I get into my truck and head home, where I take myself in my hand and come hard in my shower. I can't wait much longer.

# Chapter Nine

## LYNAE

It's been almost a week since the incident on my sofa. I want to give in and make love to him again. I miss the feeling of him inside me. I hate that I came to my senses and stopped us from going any further.

I pull up to the house where Coral and Rowdy live and wait for her to come out. JoAnna is babysitting little Archer so that Coral and I can go to town for the day. The guys are at the department doing training.

Coral walks out, dressed in jeans, cowboy boots, and a tank top with a plaid western shirt over it. I'm wearing one of my prairie dresses and my cowboy boots. It's been nice getting to know Coral. She's sweet and from Alabama. Like me, she has a southern background.

"I need to run by the station and drop off some cash for Rowdy. Are you okay with that?"

"Yeah."

We head into town. When we pull up to the fire station, I pause. Cars are stopped on the side of the road, and I see nothing but women standing around.

"Damn women complain that men make them sexual objects, yet here they are, objectifying our men."

I don't understand why the crowd of women are gathered here, until I see them. Coming out of the bay are Rowdy and Ryker, both shirtless, while the other guys are in full turnout gear. Rowdy and Ryker each have a bundle of hose draped over their shoulders. I watch as they stand at the bottom of a set of stairs. Ryker's cousin Lance steps out—also shirtless. His suspenders hang low at his hips, while Ryker and Rowdy have them over their shoulders to hold up their pants.

"Go," Lance says, and I watch as both men take off, running up the tower.

"Woohoo, go guys," a woman yells, and I turn to look at her. "Aren't those some fine specimens of men?"

She's looking at my man, ogling him.

My man.

The thought almost makes me collapse. I watch as Ryker makes it to the top of the tower with Rowdy right behind him. They laugh and chuckle as they come back down. Ryker looks over and sees me leaning against the front of my car. He drops the hose and walks over.

"Hey, baby." He laughs, and all I focus on are his muscles flexing. The sweat dripping down his impressive muscular chest. His hair plastered to his forehead.

I can't stop myself. I stand up and pull him down,

taking his lips. He takes over the kiss and wraps me up in his arms. People are whooping and hollering, but I ignore them.

"I want to go home," I say as soon as our lips part.

"On it. Let me change, and I'll be ready."

"No, I want you now," I whisper so only he can hear. His eyes flare, and he looks down at my hardened nipples.

"Damn, I thought he was free," a woman says, and I look over at her as Ryker pulls away from me.

"No, he's very much taken. See this?" I rub my belly and point to Ryker. "Mine," I tell her.

"Fuck, that's hot. I'll be right back, vixen," Ryker says before he leaves me to head back to the bay.

I don't know what he says to his lieutenant or the others, but I notice that Coral and Rowdy are gone too. My phone pings, and I look down at it.

CORAL

I'll catch a ride with Rowdy. We can hang out next weekend.

ME

Okay. I'm going home with Ryker.

Ryker returns, still shirtless, but he's in his jeans and work boots now.

"Follow me home."

I get in my car and follow him to his house. My heart clenches that he called it our home. We enter through the mudroom door, which connects to the laundry room, and head straight for the master bedroom.

"I need to shower," he says before taking my lips again. He lifts me up his body and carries me into the bathroom.

Ryker sits me on the counter and lifts my dress over my body, leaving me in my panties and bra. I kick off my boots, and he removes his boots and jeans. His cock is straining in his boxers, and I lick my lips.

"Fuck, I want your mouth on me."

I bob my head up and down, excited. I jump off the counter and strip out of my bra and panties. He pushes me into the shower stall and turns on the water. We rinse off his body before I drop to my knees and take his long, thick cock between my lips. I slide up and down his shaft a couple of times before he takes over. He thrusts in and out of my mouth. I cup his balls and squeeze them gently.

"Enough." His voice is so gravelly I almost come right then.

He's turned on as much as I am. I can feel myself leaking from my core. He pulls himself from between my lips and lifts me up. In one motion, he has me pressed into the wall and his cock inside me. I throw my head back and moan.

"Yes, Ryker. I missed you so much," I confess.

"I fucking missed this tight ass pussy."

He pumps into me, over and over. His chest hair tickles my nipples, and I wrap my hands around his shoulders and dig my fingers into his hair. He pulls out and sits on the seat before pulling me toward him. He turns me so my back is to his chest and enters me in a long thrust. I lean my head back on his shoulder as he holds my hip with one hand and helps me move over him while the other tweaks my nipples. I come hard and scream his name. He doesn't stop and keeps going. Now, both of his hands are holding my waist as he moves me up and down on him. He thrusts up, and my eyes cross as I start to come again. This time, he follows me over, and we come together.

*Ryker*

W ho knew a little bit of jealousy was all it would take? We are in my bed now, where we've made love a couple more times since the shower. She's napping in my arms, and I'm staring at the ceiling as I keep one arm wrapped around her and the other up behind my head.

I'm thinking over this last week. We've spent every day together when we were off work. At the appointment, we found out we are having a little boy. I have an ultrasound picture of him on my fridge. We also gave one to my parents in a frame. They loved it. We haven't told them that we decided on a name. I want to name him after Rowdy's father, but I want to talk to him first and make sure he's okay with that before we announce it.

Carefully, I extricate myself from Lynae's body and slip on a clean pair of boxers. I head to the kitchen to find something to make us for dinner. There's a frozen meal that my dad sent home for me. I pop it into the microwave then grab some fresh bread Mom dropped off yesterday.

By the time I have everything ready and I'm about to find a tray to carry it into the room, I turn around to see her standing there. She's in one of my shirts, and I wonder if she's completely naked under it. I'm going to have her for dessert once I'm done feeding her.

"You cooked."

"No, I warmed up food. I can cook, but everything is frozen."

"Smells good." She moves toward me, and I open my arms so I can pull her into my body. She snuggles in, and I can imagine us doing this for years to come.

"I'm sorry I didn't talk to you about changing the parameters of our relationship before I told that woman you were my boyfriend."

I lift her up onto the counter and instantly know she's bare under the shirt. I hold her face in my hands as I slide my body between her knees.

"I've been wanting our relationship to change since I met you, so I'm okay with it, babe." I kiss her lips, and before I know it, I'm sliding my boxers down to release my cock and take her on the counter.

When she cries out my name and it ricochets off the walls, my chest swells with pride.

I have to reheat our food, but then we carry it to our room and eat in bed as we discuss more about our past.

"Why did you only have sex one other time before me?" I have to know. It's a need deep in my soul. I want to know everything about her.

"Sayler basically raped me on our wedding night, and I couldn't sleep with him again after that. He tried and pushed me a couple of times, but I wouldn't let him. One time, he was holding me down." She pauses, and I watch as she shivers at the memory. "He was going to force me, but I screamed, and his dad walked into the room."

"He what?"

"Yeah, I don't think his dad had a healthy liking for me either. The whole family is a bit crazy."

"Fuck. I can't believe your father was okay giving you to them."

I watch her look down and then back up to me. "I want to be completely honest with you."

"I want that too, baby."

"My parents kidnapped me from my grammy and poppy. They'd lost custody of me and hated it. So, after Poppy died, they took me and told me my grammy was dead." Tears start rolling down her cheeks, and I pull her onto my lap. "I thought I was seeing a ghost when she showed up in Tucson."

"Baby, I'm going to make sure that the rest of your life is good."

"Thank you, honey." My heart swells at her words.

When I hold her close to me as we fall asleep, I silently pray I can always protect her and our children. I slide my hand over her belly as my eyes drift closed.

## Chapter Ten

### LYNAE

It's been over a month since I changed our relationship. We are officially boyfriend and girl-friend. However, he won't leave my side very much lately, not after Coral was kidnapped and buried alive. I try to assure him that no one is coming after me. I'm safe.

I'm twenty-five weeks pregnant and getting bigger every day. The doctor keeps saying it's because of how big Ryker is that our baby is growing so fast. I'm measuring at almost twenty-eight to thirty weeks, but developmentally, he's right on target.

Ryker is upset with me because I'm still working at the vineyard restaurant when Jaden needs me, like tonight. I move between the tables, watching the floor to make sure I don't trip on something.

"Welcome to Painted Desert Winery and Vineyard. Can I tempt you with a glass of our famous wine?" I ask the couple seated at the table.

"Lynae?"

I look up and freeze. "Hello, Mr. and Mrs. Humphreys. How are you doing?"

"You're pregnant? Cheri said the pregnancy didn't take. Does she know?"

"Oh, no, this isn't from that. I got pregnant right afterward with my boyfriend's baby."

"Lynae, you okay?" Ryker says from behind me.

I love that he can sense when I'm not feeling right. I'm freaking out because if they go back and tell Cherise and Ken I'm pregnant, it could start another court battle.

"Excuse me, sir, she's speaking to us," Mrs. Humphreys says, her tone dripping with condescension as she addresses Ryker.

"I'm her boyfriend, so back off, lady."

"Well, I never." She gasps and holds her hand to her chest like she's shocked.

"Mrs. Humphreys, let me get you a glass of wine. Mr. Humphreys, would you like me to get you some brandy? I'll also have another server help you."

I put in their drink orders and ask one of the other waitresses to help them before I join Ryker in the kitchen.

"Who are they?" he asks when I step up to him.

"They are close friends with Cherise and Ken." My heart beats faster as worry sets in.

"Who are Cherise and Ken?" Jaden asks from where he's running the kitchen and checking all the plates before they go out.

We haven't told his family about Sayler's, or the court battle I went through. I'm sure they'd look at me differently if they knew I had been on hormones and didn't protect their son or myself.

"They're Lyn's ex-in-laws," Ryker answers.

"Would you like me to send them a nice dessert?" He hasn't looked over at us to see that I'm stressing or the worried look on Ryker's face.

I lean up and whisper, "I'm scared."

I've made sure to be honest with Ryker about everything, and my feelings are the most important. We still haven't told each other how we feel about one another, but I know I'm falling in love with him.

"I'll protect you. I'll call my attorney on Monday. Can you call yours?"

"Yes."

"Kids, what aren't you telling me?" Jaden walks over and stands with us, having overheard us talking about attorneys.

"Can we talk in your office?" Ryker asks, and Jaden nods. He has the head chef take over the line before leading us into the room.

"Do I need to have your mother here?"

"Yeah, maybe, so we don't have to explain this more than once," Ryker says.

Charlene walks in a few moments later, and by this point, I've worked off a couple of pounds bouncing my leg in fear. Ryker reaches across and gently rubs my thigh.

"I got you, baby," he says, and I start to calm.

"What's going on?" his mom asks.

I take a deep breath. I need to be the one to tell them. I start by explaining how I was forced to marry Sayler and how my grandmother helped me get the divorce. Then, I tell them how, when Sayler went missing, a clause suddenly appeared in the prenup I had signed. The judge ruled that I had to undergo one round of hormones and one attempt at insemination. I explain that it didn't take, and I have the proof, not only in pregnancy tests but also in an ultrasound.

"I didn't think about the hormones still raging through my body and ended up making a bad judgement error when I met Ryker. Several weeks later, I found out I was pregnant. We know it's Ryker's. As proof, I had an amniocentesis and got the DNA results. It's not Sayler's baby. It's Ryker's." I finish. I hadn't told Ryker that part yet.

"Babe, I trusted you." He pulls me onto his lap and holds me as I cry.

"I needed to make sure that, if there was ever any question, you wouldn't lose our child. Especially if something happens to me."

"You don't trust them?" He holds my face in the palm of his hands, staring me down. I can't hide and fidget with my lip between my teeth, and he knows. "Fuck." He pulls me into him, his arms banding me close. "I'm not losing you." I can hear the fear in his voice.

"Call the attorney. We need to be prepared for them. That woman out there isn't going to keep what she saw a secret," Jaden says, standing from his desk to hold his wife.

"I can get a hold of some of my old contacts with child protective services. They can't and won't get their hands on my grandbaby. They are sick for forcing a child to marry their adult son," Charlene adds.

Charlene used to work for the state before quitting to help at the vineyard. She helped Coral when she was having issues with one of Rowdy's exes.

I don't want to be alone tonight, so Ryker stays with me at my house, holding me through the night after he makes love to me.

---

*Ryker*

I n the last couple of weeks since Lynae ran into the Humphreys, we've gotten everything put together with both of our attorneys. Mine will head up the case from here, while hers will use his staff to do some investigating for us. I'm not going to allow the Benedicts to get away with anything this time. She's told me everything they did to her in the last case. How she basically walked away with nothing just to get away from them.

To get our mind off the Benedicts, we had dinner with Rowdy and Coral tonight. Coral is still recovering from everything she went through at the end of

September and doesn't like to go out much. That's why we go to their place, or Lyn will hang out with Coral some days after school.

We pull up to Lyn's small house, and something doesn't feel right. I reach across her to open the glove box, where I keep my gun. I pull it out and slip it into the back of my waistband.

"What's that for?" Lyn's voice is high-pitched.

"Something feels off."

"I left the porch light on."

"Stay here."

"No." She tries to fight me. I dial Logan.

"What's up?" he answers, and I can hear the baby crying in the background.

"Get Mom to your house and come to Lynae's. Something isn't right."

"Don't go in," he warns, but he should know me better than that. If someone is in there, I'll kill them to protect my girl.

I pull my flashlight from the door pocket before stepping down from the truck. The wind blows through the trees, and I can smell something in the air. I hear the passenger door open.

"Stay there, Lyn," I order her and move to the porch.

The door is cracked open. I push it with my foot, and it stops part way. I change tactics and move to the side porch, just in case someone is behind the front door. I pull my gun from my waistband and hold it at my side. Trying to avoid the boards that would give away my position, I move silently toward the French doors. I can barely see into the room, not even the microwave or stove displays light up the kitchen. I reach through the broken glass and unlock the doors before opening them and stepping inside. My boots crunch on glass as I hold my gun at the ready. I flick on my flashlight and see complete disarray. Everything is destroyed. When my light bounces off of pictures in frames positioned all over the house, my blood runs cold. I back out of the room and head for my truck.

"What's wrong?" Lyn asks, and I hate to ask, but I have to know.

"Are you sure Sayler is dead?"

"Why?" Her breathing increases.

"You'll see."

We wait for my brother. When he arrives, he and I check the perimeter and find that the main power to the house has been shut off. We turn it back on and move inside, while Lyn remains secured in the truck. Once the house is cleared, Logan calls his forensics person, and I head back outside to get Lyn. She's crying, and I hold her as she sees the destruction through the window.

"Why do you think it's Sayler?" she asks.

I don't answer her question. When we step over the threshold, she sees the answer. All around the room are framed pictures from their wedding. Every surface is covered. From the pictures, I can see how young my girl was, and I also notice the fear in her eyes. I see the pure evil in his smile. I pull her close to my body as we walk through the rooms. Her clothes are strewn everywhere and cut to pieces. The baby's room, which she had started decorating, is completely demolished. Nothing was left intact, not even the appliances.

"You're moving in with me, Lyn." I don't ask, I tell her.

"Okay." She doesn't fight me on it, and I know it's because she's scared.

After we answer a few questions, I take her home. I'm glad she has a few outfits at my house so she can go to work tomorrow. I tried to talk her into staying home, but she won't. I help her into bed, and we fall asleep in each other's arms.

When she wakes up screaming in her sleep, I comfort her to calm her down.

## Chapter Eleven

### LYNAE

I've been living with Ryker for two weeks now. I love it here. I can set the alarm when he's not here, and I feel safe. I also know where all the guns are hidden. He promised he'd put them away when the baby comes, but for now, I know it's for safety.

Tonight, we have dinner plans at the restaurant with his mom and brother. I'm trying to get ready, but my hands won't stop shaking. I can't kick the feeling that I'm being watched. It's been like this all day. Ryker isn't home yet. I look across the lake to Logan's house, almost tempted to call him and see if he and Reese want to come hang out until it's time to go. But I don't want Ryker to worry about me more than he already does. Every time we make love since the break-in, he's so caring and gentle with me. I just want us to return to a semblance of normal. Maybe that's why I feel off.

The alarm beeps as someone enters the code, and I

watch as Ryker steps through the mudroom door. I'm on him before he can get his boots off. I need him so badly. My body needs some kind of release. I kiss him and try to climb up his body. He lifts me up and carries me to our room, where he lays me on the bed. He opens my robe.

"Fuck, Ly, you're beautiful." He rubs his hands across our child and then slides it down my body to my pussy, where he slips two fingers inside me. I arch and moan as he takes me higher. When he pulls his fingers away, I whimper and open my eyes. "Watch me, baby," he orders.

I love it when he gets all demanding and alpha. His cock kisses my entrance before he slides it in. He starts off with slow pumps, but I reach around and grab his butt cheek.

"Ryker, fuck me like you used to. I need it, now." My voice cracks, and he pumps in harder, holding my knees to keep me from sliding across the bed.

Because of how big I've gotten, we've had to alter how we make love. This is one of my favorite ways. He likes reverse cowgirl. Both of us like doggy style. But I really love this position. I can watch him go over, and he can slam into me hard. He does that now, and I cry out. He pauses to make sure I'm not hurt before he continues.

When I slide my fingers down my body and start playing with my clit, he groans, and his thrusts become erratic, but he's pumping harder and harder into me. I can feel myself going over, and I scream as I come hard.

I then feel the warmth of him coming inside me. He holds himself deep and then leans over me, careful not to crush my stomach.

"Marry me, Lynae. I want to do this every day for the rest of my life with you."

"No." I smile at him. "I'm not going to let you marry me just because I'm pregnant."

"I already told you, it's not about that."

"No." It's on the tip of my lips to tell him I love him, and that's what I want to hear from him before I accept his proposal.

He pulls out and helps me up. I get cleaned up and finish dressing so we can go.

———

A couple of hours later, we are sitting, enjoying our meal, when a shadow falls over the table. I look up in horror and stand to face off with her.

"Cherise, what are you doing here?"

She slaps me hard, splitting my lip. "You lying bitch. That's my grandbaby you're carrying. I'll make you sorry for keeping me from it." She slaps a sheath of papers onto the table and turns to walk away.

"Sorry, ma'am, that was assault." Logan stops her and forces her to sit down in a chair.

While we wait for the police to arrive, she verbally attacks me, calling me names. I sit there with tears rolling down my face, wondering if I should have just left town so Ryker and his family didn't have to deal with the crazy of the Benedict family.

"I shouldn't have moved here," I say, my voice barely audible.

"Don't ever say that. I love you. I've loved you since the moment I first laid eyes on you. You are mine, Lynae. I told you I'd never stop asking. I mean it," Ryker says as he storms over to me. Everyone is watching us, even Cherise.

I look up at him and stand, then I use the chair to help me kneel down before him. I don't know why I'm doing this, but he just said everything I needed to hear.

"Ryker—"

"Get up off the floor, baby." He interrupts me.

"No, let me finish." I take a deep breath as I wipe the tears from my face. "I love you too. I've loved you since then also. I shouldn't have loved you, but I did. I love you because you gave me a family and our baby." I hold out my hand for him to help me up. "Will you marry me?" I ask him, and he pulls me up with a chuckle.

"Yeah, baby, we're getting married. But remember, I asked you first." He reaches into his pocket and pulls out a ring, which he slips onto my finger. I look at it and then at him in shock.

I'm beyond surprised. "How long have you had this?"

"Since the day after you told me you were carrying my baby."

"I love you," I say before he kisses me.

"That's ridiculous. That's my son's child."

"No, it's not. We have paternity proving it," Ryker says with a little smile and puffs out his chest. He's being so smug that I can't help but laugh.

The police take Cherise to the station, where she is booked for assault.

## Chapter Twelve

### RYKER

We stand in my parents' yard, all waiting. When the doors open, my breath catches in my chest.

"Breathe," Rowdy says beside me.

I take a deep breath and watch as Lynae walks out on my dad's arm. She's wearing a dress that skims the floor with long, sheer sleeves. The skirt flows down her body, highlighting her thirty-two-week pregnant belly. Her hair, which has grown longer since we started seeing each other again, is in waves around her shoulders. She's wearing only a tiara on her head, no veil.

When she reaches me, I take her hand and pull her close to my body. I hold her the entire time as we say our vows and exchange rings. I told her I wouldn't always be able to wear a ring, but I would tattoo one for her so women would know I'm married. She slides the tungsten ring onto my finger. It's mostly plain, except for the edges, which are accented with rose gold. It complements the rose gold set with a pear-shaped diamond I got her. The only other jewelry she has on is the butterfly necklace her grammy gave her and my engagement ring.

When I slip her ring onto her finger, I pull her hand up to kiss it, then look into her eyes as I vow to protect and love her forever. She gives me the vows she wrote, and I'm more in love with her than I ever thought possible. When the officiant finally says I can kiss her, I kiss her deeply, but I want more as I pull away.

The rest of the evening is spent celebrating with our family and friends. No one brings up the looming court date on Monday that we've been struggling with. I'm still worried that Sayler is alive. Too many weird things keep happening. Not only is she being followed, but someone tried to break into my house one night. They ran off before we could get them, but I swear it was a man.

I take her home to our house, finally feeling settled for the first time in a long time. I'm shocked to see her sitting on the bed after I secure the house. She's got my shirt I wore earlier for the wedding on and nothing else. Her pregnant belly peeking out, along with the beautiful curve of her breasts. She's sitting cross-legged with her hands wrapped around our baby. I can't stop myself from taking a picture so I'll never forget this moment. She smiles at me before she bites that sexy lip and reaches out for me. It's one of the sexist things I've ever seen.

I make love to my wife, showing her how much I

love her, and then I hold her close when she falls asleep. We decided to hold off on a honeymoon until after the baby is born and a bit older. We have tonight, and then when school goes on winter break, we'll spend time together when I'm not working.

--------

*Lynae*

Sitting in the court room, I look over at the Benedicts' table. Only Cherise is there with her attorney. He stands up after the judge tells us to be seated.

"Your honor, we would like to request our own paternity be done on the baby."

The judge holds up his hand. "No. This is from an independent doctor in Flagstaff. I'm not going to contest science, and you shouldn't either. I can't believe this case came to my court."

"Your honor, we tried to have it settled before now, but the plaintiff wanted it to come to court." Our attorney defends us.

"I see that. I rule for the defendant in this case. The baby is clearly not related to the Benedict family, and they have no reason to seek custody of the unborn child. This frivolous case shouldn't have ever been brought here. It's a waste of my time." His gavel hits the stand hard, and I jump. Ryker squeezes my hand, and my lips tip up slightly as I look at him.

As soon as the judge exits, we are ready to leave.

"You'll never raise that baby. I won't allow it," Cherise threatens.

"We've already filed a restraining order against you and is currently in effect. You threaten my client again, and I will have you charged," our attorney says. "Get control of your client," he tells her attorney, and we make our way out of the courthouse and head home.

When we get back to the vineyard, we head for Ryker's parents' house. Charlene is waiting out front and takes me in her arms, hugging me tightly. They wanted to come with us to court, but because it was family court, the judge wanted only the parties involved there.

"I have a pair of your favorite fuzzy jammies waiting for you. Go get changed."

I look at Ryker and then back to his mom. "What's going on?"

"I have to work tonight, babe. Sorry. I think you should stay here at my parents', please."

"Okay." I'll give him this because we've been so stressed out, and I need him to be calm for work. I don't want him worried about me and getting hurt.

He's not working for the fire department tonight. It's one of his nights on the hospital helicopter. He's gotten on a regular schedule, working a 24-hour shift twice a week, every other week.

He kisses me goodbye, tells me how much he loves

us, and I walk into the house, which smells like fresh bread and good food. I love coming over here. His family has become my family.

***

L ast night, I slept like shit without Ryker by my side, but I'm glad I stayed here and not at our house by myself. It's cooler today, and when I step out onto the back deck, I see snowflakes gently falling. I love that living up here means we get snow in the winter. I check my phone and see a text from Ryker.

HUSBAND

I love you, baby. Relax today and enjoy the snow.

ME

I love you too. Be careful.

He doesn't respond, so I know he's busy working. The snowy conditions could mean auto accidents and more that he needs to focus on. He'll be home later today, and we'll go home together to sit on our deck and watch the snow.

***

I sit in the chair, wrapped in a blanket with another fuzzy pajama set on. I must have drifted off because I'm woken by a loud bang. I realize it's a gunshot when another goes off. I'm too big to run or hide, but I'm worried about my family. I look for my purse that has a gun in it and realize I left it in the room instead of carrying it with me. I'm not at our house, where we have guns hidden everywhere.

I stand and turn as the doors open, nearly falling over when I see Sayler walking out with Charlene in his grip. He's not clean-shaven like he used to be, and his hair is a mess. But it's the wild look in his eyes that gives me pause. He's always been a bit on edge, but this is pure insanity. His gaze moves up and down my body, finally settling on my stomach. I wrap my arms around my belly to protect my son.

"Don't hurt her, Sayler," I beg, and he hits her with the gun, dropping her to the ground as he aims it at me. I don't know what to do except do as he says to save both my baby and Charlene.

I think about Isla. She's on Christmas break, and I hope she's not in the house hurt. I haven't seen her so far today, so I assume she left or is still in bed. She didn't come in until late last night.

"Come here, wife," he orders me, and I walk to him, careful of the slippery deck. He grabs me by the hair and yanks me to his body. "You are mine."

"I thought you were dead."

He twists me around, pressing my back to his chest as he forces me toward the front of the house.

"Doesn't matter. You die too, then. We are only ever to be with each other. No one else." He sounds crazy, and his eyes are bouncing all over as if he's tripping on something.

Now is probably the wrong time to point out that he was cheating on me. I'm scared, but I can't show it. He likes weakness. I'm not the same girl I was in Tucson. I keep my chin held high and talk in a firm and level voice.

"Sayler, you need to leave. This isn't your house, and you hurt the owner. This isn't your baby; it's my husband's." Wrong thing to say. He yanks harder on my hair and pulls me up his body.

"I'll kill them all if you don't do as I say. Now, let's go. That's my child."

He drags me through the house, leaving the doors open, and pushes me into the passenger side of a Jeep. I maneuver the seat belt so it's under my belly and make sure I'm away from the dash as he walks around the car. I could jump out, but I don't want to get shot. I just hope that someone comes to help Charlene and discovers I'm missing before it's too late.

"By the way, I owe you," he says, and I turn to him in shock.

What could he possibly owe me?

His fist comes flying at me, and I can't avoid the hit. I feel my nose break as blood starts dripping down it, and my head ricochets back, slamming into the window as my eyes drift close, sending me into unconsciousness.

## Chapter Thirteen

### RYKER

I land the helicopter at the station as my brother pulls up. I don't know why he demanded I meet him here, but I'm free to take a short break. Maybe he brought my wife with him so I can see her. I watch him step out of his SUV. The only person with him is Rowdy. Lance comes out of the firehouse and walks toward us.

They all have tight expressions. My brother's eyes are hidden behind a pair of aviator sunglasses. Rowdy is the one I can read the best. I see the anger in his clenched jaw and the way he keeps flexing his fists. It's similar to what he did when Coral was taken. I look around us, but I don't see anyone else. The ambulance bay is empty. They must be out on a run.

"Lynae is in labor?" The thought hits me.

Logan shakes his head, and I watch as his head drops.

"No," I say. I won't believe something happened to

her. I promised. I left her with my parents, where she was safe. "Mom and Dad?"

"Dad is okay. He left for a bit because there was an emergency at the restaurant. We think it was a setup," Logan says, and I take a step back, knowing what's coming. "It's a good thing that when the gunshots went off, Isla hid in her room. He didn't find her. Mom was pistol-whipped and is on the way to the hospital. But he took Lynae."

"No," I bellow, turning to swing at something, but nothing is close by. "He who?" I ask, already knowing the answer deep in my gut.

"You were right. It's her ex-husband. He's alive. The military police are on their way, along with the state police."

Logan shows me images from our parents' security camera. Sayler has Lyn by the hair, dragging her toward a Jeep. The next picture shows the car pulling away, and my wife is slumped against the window, her eyes closed. I can make out the blood on her face and know he hit her. I'm going to kill the fucker.

"Where did he take her?"

"We don't know," Rowdy says, and I look out over the mountains surrounding us. They could be anywhere.

"How the fuck am I supposed to find her out there?" I swing my arms wide in frustration.

"You can. You will," Rowdy says as he wraps an arm around my shoulders. "You got this. We have some things to look over."

"How long ago did this happen?"

"A couple of hours ago."

"And I'm just now being told?"

"We got a hold of you as soon as we could. I've been running down a lot of information in the meantime. Plus, we did some local searching, hoping we could get to her before we had to call you." Logan defends the decision to wait, but I'm beyond pissed.

"He took my fucking pregnant wife, brother. There is no waiting. I should have been notified as soon as you found out."

"We have video footage from the cameras around the vineyard. I was able to track the car through town and out but lost it in the mountains," Logan adds, and I finally realize what I need to do.

"I'll call and get another pilot to take over my shift. You"—I point at Lance—"make the call to activate search and rescue. I'll take the helicopter and start a grid pattern search around the area where you lost the car." I gesture toward the joint fire station and sheriff's office helicopter, which is used by search and rescue when needed.

"I'll call in everyone we know to help," Rowdy offers, and I nod at him as I step away to make the call.

With a new pilot enroute, I look over the map, comparing it to the video footage and street camera sightings. Together with the other members of the search and rescue team that I'm a part of, we come up with a plan. We found footage in town of the car turning up a road leading toward the trailhead where hikers typically head. The Prominence trailhead has several cabins along the way. We have a direction now. I need a clear plan so that when I get into the helicopter, I'm not just searching randomly. The other members head out in their trucks to begin their ground searches.

The helicopter lifts off, and I'm glad to have my mind focused on getting my wife back. Both Logan and Lance decided to come with me, likely because they're afraid of what I'll do. They saw Rowdy hand me a gun. I'm not going to let that man think he can take my wife. She's not his anymore. He fucked that up, and I was there to pick up the pieces and help build her up again.

---

*Lynae*

I come to and instantly know something is wrong. My body feels fuzzy and exposed. I look down and scream. I'm lying on a bed, blood and fluids staining the area around my lower body, but that's not why I'm crying. My legs are tied to the posts of the bed, keeping me open on stirrups. I'm naked, and then I realize my water broke. My hands clutch at my stomach as a contraction hits me. I spot the IV pole and the line inserted into my arm. I try to pull it out, but my head swims when I sit up. What are they pumping into my veins?

I don't know how long I've been unconscious or

what they gave me, but I don't feel right. Everything is dulled, and I'm slow to respond.

"Stop it right now," Cherise yells, and I tilt my head back to see Sayler standing behind her. "No one can hear you." She walks over and examines my exposed body. "Almost ready. Breaking her water after you drugged her up was perfect. Our baby will be here soon, son. Then we can finally get rid of her."

"Yes, Mama."

He looks at her, and bile rises in my throat. It's a twisted, sick look of affection. I knew there was something off between them, but I never could have imagined this. She smiles at me with a sinister grin before turning and pulling Sayler closer.

"You guessed it. My son loves me very much. You were just a means to an end. I will kill for our love, and so will he. Just yesterday, we finally got rid of that pawing asshole father of his." She chuckles, and I turn my head and vomit. "Stop being a big baby. It's the way it should be. A son should love his mother above all other women. She teaches him what a woman wants and needs."

Sayler wraps his arms around her, and my body shakes in revulsion. She starts to laugh.

"Do you know what I did when your grandmother found us?"

"No. No. That's not possible." I cry harder as I think of my grammy.

"Being a former nurse, I knew exactly how to make

it look like a natural death. A perfect bubble of air placed just right in her vein."

"Nurses are supposed to help and heal people."

"We do. I just couldn't have her revealing the fact that my son was alive, not missing. I helped him escape. I paid the right people to make it look like an attack on his unit, and then they put him in hiding. Enough money will buy you just about anything. I even paid some actors to portray beheading Sayler so he wouldn't be considered AWOL."

"What?" It was all a setup. She's a sick individual, but so is her son. "Sayler, don't do this. Just let me and my baby—" I stop as a hard contraction hits me, and I feel the urge to push. "Please don't do this," I beg him, but there is nothing in his eyes.

Cherise and Sayler stand there for a moment longer and then get to work. My son is born roughly thirty minutes later. It's so painful. I feel like I'm being torn in half. I try to fight against the restraints as my baby makes a soft cry. I'm scared he's not strong enough. He's four weeks early, and the labor could have been too fast for him. Cherise cleans him up, and his cries become louder. I pray Ryker finds him.

"Please don't take him. He's my baby. Please," I beg, over and over. I scream and cry right along with him.

Cherise hands the baby over to Sayler and walks over to me. She starts pushing something into my IV, and I feel a sudden coldness spread through my veins.

"Take him to the car, my love. I'll take care of her."

She looks away from me, and I pull the IV away

from her hand. I scream and fight her as Sayler walks out. I get a grip of her clothes and rip them. She drops the syringe in our struggle. I grab it and stab it into her leg. Cherise screams as I push the plunger. Whatever fate she left me to, she'll face it too. I realize that she only got a small amount into me, but I've gotten a full dose into her.

She falls to the floor as Sayler rushes back into the room. She's watching me but doesn't do anything. She lifts her arm, but it falls back to her side, and she just stares at me.

I'm sitting up now, untying my feet from the ropes and stirrups they installed on the bed. Breaking a stirrup free, I swing at Sayler when he gets close. My baby is nowhere in sight. The metal hits him, and I roll for the other side of the bed. I hit something on the floor and rear back when I look into Ken's sightless eyes. His corpse is shoved under the bed, along with something else—my possible salvation.

"Come back here, you bitch. What did you do to her?" Sayler comes around the bed.

I lift the gun that was beside Ken and pull the trigger. It fires, and blood blooms on Sayler's chest. My baby cries from the other room. Cherise makes a gurgling sound as Sayler falls to the floor. I stand up on shaky legs and use the bed and wall to get out of the room. I step over Sayler's dead body and ignore Cherise as she mumbles shit at me. In the main room of the cabin, I find my son strapped into a car seat. There's a phone sitting on the table next to him.

I dial the number and pray he answers.

"Who is this?"

My legs are getting weaker. Blood flows from between my legs, and I start to get dizzy. The need to protect my child overwhelms me. I look around at my surroundings and out the window. I can see the sign for the trailhead. I know what cabin we are in. Ryker pointed it out to me one time when we came up here for a drive.

"Ryker, help him. They forced me to deliver him." Gently, I take JJ from the car seat and walk to the sofa. I don't have much energy left in my body. I lie down and turn so he's protected between me and the sofa as I give him my breast. There's a blanket on the back of the sofa that I pull over our bodies.

"We are at the old Forest Service Cabin. Hurry, I don't know how much longer I can keep him warm."

"Lyn, I'm on my way. Where is Sayler?"

"Killed him, but Cherise could come to."

"I'm landing now."

"I love…you." I barely get the words out before succumbing to the darkness. I can hear my name being screamed, but I just pray that JJ is safe.

## Chapter Fourteen

### RYKER

We are out of the helicopter and running for the cabin. I'm glad there was a big enough spot in the parking lot for me to put down. I beat my brother and cousin to the door, ready to kick it in, but then I remember that night when Lyn collapsed. Instead of rushing in, I twist the knob as they come up behind me. Carefully, I push the door open. My eyes land on Cherise standing in the doorway of a room, a gun aimed directly at me. I react and fire at the same time as Logan. Her body falls backward, and I see the blood trail on the floor.

Turning, I find my wife unconscious on the sofa. I rush to her and drop to my knees. Gently rolling her, I see our son nursing at her breast, but her breathing is shallow. I check her pulse. It's faint. She's naked, and I notice blood pooling around her. Pulling back the blanket, I look to see if she's been shot, but instead, I find the blood is coming from between her thighs. She could be hemorrhaging.

"Call the air ambulance," I command. I won't be able to fly her myself. I'm too worried about her.

By the time the paramedics arrive, my concern has shifted to both my son and wife. He isn't crying much, and he's barely nursing at all. I hope he's just falling asleep, exhausted from nursing and the stress of his early birth. After attaching monitors to Lynae, the paramedics strap her to the board. I carry my son to the waiting chopper and climb up next to the crew.

We make it to Flagstaff within minutes, and I'm relieved to see both of them still alive. The nurses take JJ from my arms and lead Lynae away from me. I begin pacing, the weight of everything pressing down on me, as my brother and the rest of my family arrive.

"Sayler and Cherise are dead. We also found Ken's body. He's been dead for a while." Logan informs me.

"Good riddance," I say, not wanting to think of what they did to my wife before she killed them.

We wait. I'm on the verge of losing it when a doctor finally walks in. He pulls off his surgical cap, and we approach him.

"They are both alive. Mrs. Murphy had fentanyl in her system, along with oxytocin. Her labor was quick and intense, so we'll need to monitor her for any effects. We checked for a rupture or any retained placenta causing the bleeding. It was just trauma from the speed at which labor was induced. We'll have to wait and see if there are any long-term effects that could impact her ability to have more children, but we're hopeful. She is strong and should recover." He looks directly at me. "Your son is also very strong. He's small but would've been a larger baby if he'd made it to full term. We have him under observation as well. We cleaned him up and will be monitoring him for lung and virus issues."

"When can I see them?"

My mother pats my arm as Isla wraps her arms around me, giving me their support.

"They are being moved to a room right now. You'll be able to go up there in a bit."

"Thank you." I shake his hand and then turn for my mother to hug me too. I'm scared and worried about the future, but I'm so damn glad they are both alive.

---

My head rests at her hip as I look up her body, watching her chest rise and fall. I don't know if this fear will ever leave me. At least I didn't have to watch paramedics give my wife CPR like Rowdy had to with Coral. Watching her bleed out was horrifying enough.

Her face is soft as she sleeps. The doctor reset her nose, and she has bruising under her eyes from Sayler hitting her. I'm glad my girl sent him to hell. She took the choice out of my hands; otherwise, I would have drawn his death out. The need to torture him has been great.

I watch as Lyn's eyes flutter and her face screws up. I touch her arm, and she jolts awake with a scream.

"Ryker, Jared," she yells, her voice hoarse.

"I'm here, baby." I reassure her. She turns panicked eyes on me as her hands go to her nearly flat stomach, and she cries harder. "Shh, baby." I stand up and place my hands on her cheeks, trying to get her focus on me. "He's right here, sleeping." Her eyes bounce around the room until she sees Isla holding him. My sister and parents haven't left my side.

"I tried. I fought them, but they drugged me. They took him from me."

"I know, sweetheart. You are amazing. You are both alive because of you. Even my mom is alive because of you." Her eyes focus on my father, who is holding Mom in his arms as she cries.

"Jared." Lyn turns back to Isla.

"The baby's name is Jared?" My father chokes on the words.

I keep a hold of my wife as I slip onto the bed with her. Isla hands her Jared, and she holds him to her chest.

We both look at my dad. "Cat's out of the bag. His name is Jared Jaden Murphy—JJ for short. We talked to Rowdy, and he loved it."

"I do too." He coughs to cover his emotion, but I can see the tears in his eyes.

"Uncle Jared was watching over him today," I say.

"Yes." My dad agrees. "He sure was."

"Are they both dead?" Lyn asks the room. "Am I in

trouble for shooting him and dosing Cherise with what-ever she put in my IV."

"No, you aren't in trouble." Logan steps into the room, holding Reese. "Yes, they're both dead. Cherise was shot, but the massive load of fentanyl she was trying to give you would have killed her regardless."

"I didn't shoot Cherise."

"I did," both Logan and I say in unison.

"She was going to shoot us. We fired faster than she could. We didn't know she was drugged up," I tell her as I hold her closer.

"Now that we know you're going to be okay, we're going to head out. We'll see you tomorrow. We love you, daughter." My dad leans over and kisses her fore-head. Everyone else hugs her and tells her how glad they are that she's alive.

As the door closes, she starts nursing Jared and tips her head back. "I love you, Ryker. Thank you for saving us both."

"I'll go to hell to save you, baby." I kiss her deep and hard so that she knows I'm serious.

*Epilogue*

LYNAE

## OVER FIVE YEARS LATER

I look out at the lake, where Ryker is playing with our children as they dance around his legs, splashing water at him. Jared holds his sister's hand since she's only three and her vest makes it harder for her to move around in. Having been in swim lessons since he was six months old, he doesn't need a vest at the lake's edge. But we make him wear one when he goes to the dock as the water is deeper there.

Jared has no lasting effects from being born early. In fact, he's bigger than most of the kids in his preschool class and will be starting kindergarten this fall. I'm not currently teaching, but I help as a substitute when they need it. I enjoy being home with my kiddos.

Ryker had insisted I see the same counselor Coral did after her ordeal. It's helped me get over a lot of the trauma. I still don't like to be away from Ryker for too long. During my pregnancy with Ester, I suffered from panic attacks and wouldn't leave the house without him. I was terrified someone might try to take her from me too. Thankfully, those fears have eased, but a part of me still holds on to that anxiety.

My husband turns to look up at me and waves. I stand from the lounger I've been relaxing on and rub my hand across my blossoming belly, where our youngest is "still baking," as Ryker calls it. This pregnancy has been less frightening than the last. I'm applying the tools my counselor taught me, focusing on the good. My family is healthy, and I'm loved like I've never been before. Ryker makes sure, every day, to tell me over and over that he loves me. He includes me in every decision and makes us his priority.

I think of everything my grammy and poppy tried to teach me and strive to live each day fully.

The End

I really appreciate you reading Grid Search. Please don't forget to leave a review. To continue reading more from Prominence Point Rescue, grab the first book in the series here, Confined Space.

Coming next year is Hostage Situation. For a complete list of my books, along with series lists and reading orders on my website.

You might want to consider signing up for E.M.'s Consent for Suspense for a free story as well as first chance at cover reveals, releases, contests and more.

*Hostage Situation*

SNEAK PEEK

Meadow

Walking down the long driveway, I head to the main office of the vineyard. I have a meeting with Charlene and Logan Murphy. I need this job. My brother decided he needed to be free and took off, leaving me with over fifty thousand dollars of debt—his debt. The car was just repossessed, which is why I'm on foot.

I took the bus from Phoenix to Prominence Point, where my friend Isla is from. I had to drop out of college because I couldn't afford it anymore. Plus, my brother stole any money I had from my scholarships.

I pull open the office door to the sound of a baby crying and see a beautiful woman trying to calm her. She bounces the baby on her hip while arguing into the phone.

"Logan Joseph Murphy, get your butt here, now. I

can't interview your nanny without you," she says into the phone, keeping her voice steady. I hear someone arguing back. "Reese is your child, son." She pauses, listening to his response. "Damn." She shakes her head. "Darn it. I'm hiring her if she's as good as Isla says. I'll set her up at your house, but if you fire this one, I'm done." She huffs and hangs up, clearly not listening to anything further. The woman turns to see me standing there.

"Let me help you." I set my backpack on a chair and reach for the crying toddler, who immediately stops when I press her to my chest. She grabs onto my braid and tries to pull it toward her mouth. "No, no, sweet girl. You don't want that." I flick the long plait over my shoulder and turn to look at the woman. "I'm Meadow Lancaster. I guess this is a live-in position?"

"Oh, yeah. I'm sorry. Isla didn't tell you that? I'm Charlene Murphy, by the way. That's Reese, my grand-daughter."

"She mentioned it could be." This changes every-thing. It's a single dad, not a couple.

"Will that work for you?"

I don't want to tell her how desperate I am. "It will be fine. I'm between places right now."

"My son is a deputy sheriff, so he's on call a lot. She doesn't normally go to strangers." Charlene waves a hand toward Reese and me.

I chuckle softly. "My family used to call me the baby whisperer. I've always loved children."

"You have the job. I've gone over your resume. I called your references, and they all said good things about you."

The door swings open behind me, and I turn to see a tall, dark-haired man with striking blue eyes. He's handsome, but there's a "don't mess with me" look on his face as he takes me and his daughter in. I know this is Logan by the sheriff uniform. His scowl is deep, lips pinched tight. A dark scruff of beard and mustache is trimmed close to his face, and his hair is shaved on the sides and spiked on top. He's muscular and broad.

"Logan, this is Meadow."

He looks at his mom and then back at me.

"See, you got it. I've got to get back to work." His voice is deep and gruff.

My nipples pebble and my core throbs, liking the sound of his voice. I watch as he turns and walks out the door. I try to shake off my thoughts, realizing it's clear I'm the only one feeling any attraction here.

---

Logan

I'm so fucked. The beautiful redhead holding my daughter is mine, but I won't go there. I can't. The last woman I trusted tried to sell my child to human traffickers.

I storm to my SUV, trying to block out the look I saw

in her green eyes. I want to drop to my knees right here and thank God above for her.

Fuck!

More from *Hostage Situation* soon.

# About E.M. Shue

E.M. Shue is an Alaskan award-winning romance author. She writes in many different sub-genres but always features badass heroines in gritty situations. As the mother to three grown daughters and two grand-daughters she wants readers to be able to see that tough girls can have happy endings too. She is married to the love of her life of over twenty-five years who she married within months of starting to date, instalove is real.

She published her first book in 2017 after having a dream that later became the Beverley Award winning, Sniper's Kiss. Since her debut, she has gone on to win this award three more times with different books and has published over fifty titles. E.M.'s goal is to always give her readers heroines that are real and heroes who make their blood pump faster.

Join E.M.'s Consent for Suspense to be kept up to date on all her new releases and appearances.

https://bit.ly/EMConsentforSuspense

E.M. SHUE

*Heroes* THAT COULD SAVE THEMSELVES BUT DON'T NEED TO

Also by E.M. Shue

### Securities International Series

Sniper's Kiss: Book 1 ~ Angel's Kiss: Book 2 ~ Tougher
Embrace: Book 2.5 ~ Love's First Kiss: Book 3 ~ Secret's Kiss:
Book 4 ~ Second Chance's Kiss: Book 5 ~ Sniper's Kiss
Goodnight: Book 5.5 ~ Identity's Kiss: Book 6 ~ Hope's Kiss:
Book 7 ~ Forever's Embrace: Book 7.5 ~ Justice's Kiss: Book
8 ~ Duchess's Kiss: Book 9 ~ Kiss of Submission: Book 9.5 ~
Precious Kiss: Book 9.75 ~ Truth's Kiss: Book 10 ~ Kiss of
Secret's Past: Book 10.5 (Coming Soon)

### Knights of Purgatory Syndicate

A Seductive Beauty ~ A Tortured Temptress ~ A Temptation
Too Great

### Santa Claus, Indiana Stories

Coal for Kiera ~ Hanna's Valentine ~ Hailey's Rodeo

### Mafia Made

Her Empire: Mafia Made 2 ~ His Rebel: Mafia Made 5 ~ Her
Exile: Mafia Made 8

## Caine & Graco Saga

Accidentally Noah ~ Zeke's Choice ~ Lost in Linc ~
Completely Marco ~ Jackson Revealed ~ Trusting Jericho

## Tattoos & Sin Series

Doctor Trouble ~ Vegas Jackpot ~ Doctor Sinful ~ Frozen
Heart ~ Doctor Do-Over ~ Rushed Decision ~ Swinging
into Love

## Stand-alones

Until Tucker: Happily Ever Alpha World ~ Discovering
Tyler ~ Until Lydia: Happily Ever Alpha World ~ Artfully
Bred ~ Rushing Her

## Caine & Graco Spin-Offs

Rocco's Atonement ~ Distracting David ~ Taliah's Warrant
Officer ~ Forever Finn's Kisses

## Devil's Handmaidens - Alaska

Wrecked ~ Off Balance ~ Rattled ~ Ruined

## Ramsey University Series

Virtuous ~ Tenacious ~ Ambitious

## Russian Cardroom Series

Ante ~ Drawing Dead ~ All In ~ Bluff

**Prominence Point Rescue Series**

Confined Space ~ Grid Search

**Shiver of Chaos**

Gambit's Property ~ Hemingway's Creed

**Granite Peak Grizzlies MC**

Aftershock's Fury (Coming June 2025)

46162075R00095